倍斯特出版事業有限公司
Best Publishing Ltd.

雅思
寫作聖經

小作文

韋爾 ◎ 著

QRCODE DOWNLOAD
英式發音

易於速成，**百變佳句** 轉瞬深印腦海
巧取 **8.0高分**

別出心裁的選字，內建高分語彙

盡數學全圖表題**高分精要**，**事半功倍**投考官所好，穩操勝卷地考取小作文**8.0高分**。

改善背誦死記式的學習，優化理解和組織能力

詳盡的引導，細說作文的構句和段落安排，輔以**高分語句和音檔**，迅速融會貫通，口說和寫作能力亦同步飆升。

PREFACE 作者序

　　仔細檢視劍橋雅思官方題本後方所提供的圖表題小作文範文，馬上能發現在這些 5-6.5 分的考生範文中都有許多共通點，在字彙和句型等運用能力的限制，使得呈現的文章表達得不夠清晰和具體，也有許多在數值等的傳遞上有許多改進點，而與 7 分以上的寫作分數失之交臂。

　　雅思寫作大、小作文的搭配使得其和雅思口說一樣，讓考生獲取 7 分以上的人大幅減少了，儘管這些考生在聽力和閱讀的分數都得到了 8-9 分。當中原因有很多，包含了小作文影響了考生獲取雅思寫作高分的穩定度。因為大多數考生擅長的都是線條圖、直線圖和圓餅圖等易於描述的主題，如果突然遇到了流程圖、遊樂園位置圖、地圖題或消防走道圖，就會因為太難發揮且不知道該使用哪些較進階的字彙去描述，以致於此次的考試分數比前一次降了 0.5-1 分，而必須要重考一次。還有很重要的一點是，不論考生的字彙量為何，都面臨一個難點，也就是考試當下腦海中所浮現能描述的字彙直接決定了考試分數。例如，描述圖表數值的增加或減少時，使用了 increase 或 decrease 一路用到底。有些儘管背過高階字彙，但又礙於不敢使用、不知是否正確，以及老師們所教授的「要用自己熟悉的字彙必免誤用」，儘管這些論點並沒有錯，但卻間接導致了繼續使用 increase 或

decrease 這些字，而繼續獲取同樣的分數段。

　　事實是，如果你沒有規律地使用這些圖表題字彙，你極可能看到圖表時，完全不知道要如何描述圖表，且倉促的完成一篇小作文，因為你必須要在 20 分鐘內完成 150-200 字的文章。這也是規劃這本小作文書籍的用意。在前一本《一次就考到雅思寫作 7+》中，確實介紹了部分小作文字彙，而且運用得宜的話也能獲取高分。但是可能對於初、中階考生來說就不是那麼完善。這次精選了許多關鍵高分字彙和片語（關於這部分可以看詳盡的目次），更能充分協助考生應對龐大的題庫並將許多關鍵字都運用上，且這些字在描述股價或求職都助益匪淺。例如，考生或許都知道描述數值跌幅很大，但卻並未使用上力道足夠的「銳減」，以及搭配多樣化的句式來獲取考官青睞。考生必須要能達到每句話都具體明確且用上書中所陳列的字彙。

　　另外要說明的是，小作文的選題，這次有選了六個題目。有鑑於考生對於單一圖表題都很擅長作答了，所以單一圖表題的部分就沒有呈現了。在《一次就考到雅思寫作 7+》也沒有呈現單一圖表題。而關於圓餅圖題，在該本寫作書呈現出較靈活的試題，例如三個圓餅圖題時的答法，也呈現過劍橋雅思 15 出現過的遊樂場地圖題，並加以更

改成更靈活的兩個時間點的雙遊樂場圖表題，以檢視考生對於時態等的掌握，且更具鑑別度。關於其他上一本提過的書籍就不再介紹了。

　　這本書的革新是，納入了雙圖表的時事題、看圖說故事題、並且維持了舊有考官會考的流程圖題。關於流程圖的部分就能看書籍中所收錄的韓國泡菜製作流程圖題。最後要講述的是關於解析和雙圖表時事題的答題方式。有別於坊間寫作書籍的呈現，書籍中的作文題均包含了解析，解析包含了引導和切入點，讓考生能迅速下筆開始寫。以關於新冠疫情的雙圖表題來看，考生就必須針對以下這八點 ❶ social distancing ❷ lockdown ❸ cases ❹ herd immunity threshold ❺ reinfection rate ❻ age 6-12 ❼ unvaccinated adults ❽ deaths driven by（delta or omicron），來進行描寫和分析，難點在於要如何寫出陳述具體的單句來描述新冠疫情（封鎖的部分，是部分封鎖，還是完全封鎖，又要如何搭配表達呢？又或者是描述未接種疫苗的成人數值或比例跟疫情變化之間的關係等等的）、適時的比較各個國家之間的數據以及如何總結這些資訊，關於這些部分，書中的解析都有做出引導，而非僅只提供考生範文。（另外要說明的是，書中的時事題的數值都是用於模擬情境，以供演練，並非實際所發生的情況。）像這類的試題和看圖說故事的題型，在英語學測中也會偶爾出現，外

加現在大考英文只考一次，相信這本書除了對雅思寫作的考生有助益之外，也能協助許多目標放在考取前段國立或醫科的考生，一次就考取理想的英文成績。最後祝所有考生都能獲取理想的分數。

韋爾　敬上

Instructions 使 | 用 | 說 | 明

整合能力強化 ❷ 單句中譯英演練

❶ 在 Table a，疫情期間，Country A 具有 7 次的完全封鎖，總計達 175 天，為世界上任何國家中封鎖日期最長的，而 Country F 卻有最少次數的封鎖，有著社交距離的減少和部分封鎖。

【參考答案】
In Table a, Country A had 7 full lockdowns during the pandemic, summing up 175 days, the most of any country in the world, whereas Country F had the least lockdown and was left with reduced social distancing, partial lockdown.

❷ 從所提供的資訊顯示，在六個國家中，Country F 過去是唯一一個仍只有第一波疫情的國家，而其他國家卻顯示出案例激增且有超過一波的疫情。

【參考答案】
From the information supplied, Country F was the only one still in the first wave among all six countries, while others exhibited surging in cases for more than once.

❸ 為了抑制進一步的疫情爆發，新冠疫情的群體免疫門檻可能與擴大的社交距離和完全封鎖有高度的相關。

【參考答案】
To curb the further outbreak, the covid-19 herd immunity threshold might be highly related to enlarged social distancing and full lockdowns.

❹ 也值得注意的是，新的變異株 omicron 的威脅讓人們感到擔憂。

【參考答案】
Also remarkable is the fact that the new variant omicron's threat made people concerned.

❺ 總結來說，儘管不同的國家經歷著不同樣的案例激增和死亡，不論是由 delta 或是 omicron 引起的，再次感染率均維持恆定，擺動於百分之五十五與六十二之間。

【參考答案】
In conclusion, despite the fact that different countries were encountering different surging in cases and death driven by either delta or omicron, reinfection rates remained constant, vacillating between 55% to 62%.

「中譯英」規劃
修正背單字盲點，背字彙亦要能造句
大幅提升考生寫作自學能力，迅速獲取高分

- 除了閱讀例句外，多了一道中譯英檢視，能觀看中文後造出文法無誤的圖表題句子，即是邁向段落寫作的第一步，改善許多記憶和量化的選擇題試題學習模式，考生自學即能循序漸進寫出圖表題佳作。

圖文呈現，精選「69 個」高分詞彙
搭配百變佳句，且每句均具體表達
一次就考取雅思寫作 8.0 以上得分

● 納入更多考生更難掌握的圖表題字彙，並協助考生內
化這些關鍵字彙，在表達數值等描述時，即刻使用各
種變化的句型並具體描述，一次就獲取考官青睞。

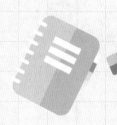

【8. escalation 上漲；增加】

■ Due to the recent **escalation** in vegetable prices, most restaurants have decided to reduce ingredients, such as tomatoes, in the dish.

Escalation

由於近期蔬菜價格的上漲，大多數餐館已經決定要在菜餚中減少像是番茄的佐料。

【還能怎麼說】

■ Meanwhile, other countries are trying to control the **escalation** in food prices for fear that there will be a protest on the street.

與此同時，其他國家正試圖控制食物價格的上漲，唯恐在街上將有抗議出現。

■ Due to an **escalation** of tulip yields in the local area, flower shop owners suspended some overseas shipments.

由於當地鬱金香產量的增加，花店店主中止了一些海外的運輸。

【9. tick up 上漲；上升】

■ Despite the fact that revenue of rare aquamarine spiders **ticked up** 25% to US 600 dollars, investors still had concerns about the fluctuation of the prices in the past few weeks.

Tick up

儘管稀有的海藍色蜘蛛的收益上漲了25%來到 600 美元，投資客對於過去幾周價格的波動仍感到擔憂。

【還能怎麼說】

■ The financial analysis report suggests that more advertising won't **tick up** the price, so companies have to think outside the box.

財政分析報告建議更多的廣告不會讓價格有所上升，所以公司必須要跳脫框架思考。

■ In September, food prices began **ticking up** unusually fast in suburb areas, making fruit farmers jubilant.

在九月，物價在郊區開始異常快速地上漲，讓水果農們興高采烈。

Instructions 使｜用｜說｜明

單字試題規劃
掌握文法和其他字彙的運用能力
提升其他單項的分數

- 加入字彙試題，額外強化圖表字彙所沒介紹，但亦非常重要的字彙，協助考生在記憶相關圖表題字彙時，也掌握例句中各種字彙，更萬全的應對雅思考試，並提升其他三個單項的分數。

📖 **Unit 1**

Questions 1-14 Complete the summary

Fruit sales have tripled to 9 million dollars, but profits **1.** _____ _____ .

Best Clothing is **2.** _____ with 5 million in **3.** _____ debts, and its shares have also sagged to a new low, according to the news.

The owner of the Best Precious Stone announced recently that **4.** _____ at the sagging archaeological site had cost 5 billion financial losses, equivalent to all investors' money.

The latest released game **5.** _____ will account for at least 35% of the overall profits in 2023.

Best Circus previously **6.** _____ 67% of garter snake exports, but a rival company has come up with an **7.** _____ strategy.

Green **8.** _____ ribbon snakes will generate 6 billion in economic output, accounting for 78% of Best Aquarium's operating **9.** _____ .

During the fiscal year, Best Automobile's overseas profits **10.** _____ at 70 million dollars, whereas its rival stood at 1 billion.

Best Automobile's **11.** _____ profits stood at 5 million dollars, and foreign investors has not shown the slightest interest in the **12.** _____ firm.

雅思百變圖表題字彙

By the time the CEO of the Best Circus accepted the job at another **13.** _____ firm, he had already sold 25% **14.** _____ _____ of the Best Circus, the share which stood at a new high of 75.9.

中階精選小文章範文

Boxes

A accounted for	**B** consoles
C fluorescent	**D** undercutting
E peaked	**F** languishing
G lumbered	**H** outstanding
I flatlining	**J** miscalculations
K sagged	**L** lucrative
M shares	**N** expenditures

參考答案

1. K	2. G	3. H	4. J	5. B	6. A	7. D
8. C	9. N	10. E	11. I	12. F	13. L	14. M

Part 2 雅思精選小作文範文

UNIT 02 雙表格題：新冠疫情時事題

Writing Task 1

You should spend about 20 minutes on this task

The diagram below includes two tables: table a and table b. Table a contains four major components related to COVID-19, whereas table b includes other information about COVID-19.

Compare and contrast about past situations in six countries and help readers get the general information by using these figures.

Write at least 150 words

整合能力強化 ❶ 實際演練

請搭配左頁的題目和下方的圖片進行圖表題寫作的演練。

Table a: COVID 19/2021/11/30

country	social distancing	lockdown	cases (wave/surging)	herd immunity threshold
A	increased	full/7/175 days	third wave	75%
B	diminished	partial/2/50 days	second wave	45%
C	enlarged	total/5/160 days	third wave	85%
D	enlarged	full/6/150 days	third wave	80%
E	decreased	partial/3/50 days	second wave	60%
F	reduced	partial/1/20 days	first wave	45%

Table b: COVID 19/2021/11/30

country	reinfection rate	age 6-12	unvaccinated adults	Deaths driven by
A	62%	eligible	40%	delta
B	60%	unqualified	80%	omicron
C	55%	eligible	35%	delta
D	58%	ineligible	45%	delta
E	56%	qualified	70%	omicron
F	55%	unqualified	70%	omicron

Part 2 雅思精選小作文範文

圖表題小作文加入時事題
游刃有餘應對龐大的雅思題庫
並有效將學習點運用在各種題目上

- 在面對某些試題時，確實容易腦筋空白或發現背誦過的許多能用於表達數值的圖表題高階字彙，在有些題目使用不上，書中小作文改善了這樣的情況，加入時事等變化題型，提升考生應對出其不意的考題，不花第二次報名費就考好寫作。

目次 CONTENTS

15 │ lag / rise / fall

■ 政府債卷持續性地落後其他債卷，動物園落後更甚、造成股票有顯著下跌，馬戲團股票持續的下跌、成長的優勢逐漸減弱

■ 水族館已經上升了 25%、股票分析師慫恿人們投資更多，數量升至 54%、多虧保健專家，龍蝦的數量在近期有顯著的增幅

■ 健康照護的股份降至 2.5，來到了最低點，科技股受到拋售的風險日益增加、預期會跌至至少 12.5%，金融股下跌

16 │ hefty / outstanding / mediocre

■ 獲得可觀的 12.5%的回報、比起特定的存款組合利率要來得高，僅小部分有可觀的效果，投資客每個月會獲得 28%的可觀利潤

■ 股份平均有顯著的 25.5%利潤，有顯著效果的抗體以移除毒性，大約 47%接種率、顯示出對肺部疾病有明顯改善

■ 遊樂園的回報率平均有平平無奇的 3.5%、對投資感到猶豫不決，診斷出的案例開始下滑後、股價約在一年後有反彈，取消訂單對銷售一般的公司是雪上加霜

17│sluggish / improve / slash

- 稀有昆蟲的市場已遲緩，當中有半數沒有顯示出遲緩的表現，症狀包含了緩慢地行走、接續的急促心臟衰竭
- 薪資在 2016 年間有著 25%的增長、其品質卻僅只有 3.5%的改進，僅有 5%的人持有外幣，到了 2016 年 11 月比率升至 15%
- 價格顯著地大幅削減 70%，產量大幅削弱了 25 萬噸、等同於歐洲出口量的 25%，這些金色螃蟹的利潤有顯著的大幅削減

18│quadruple / climb / dwindle

- 投資古怪的昆蟲成長了四倍來到 100 億元，多數的蛇咬傷都發生於十歲以下的小孩、這個月的總數已經增加了四倍，果農預期利潤會增加四倍
- 期待利潤會在 2025 年攀升至另一個高峰，黃金價格攀升至四個月的高點，高收益債卷即將要推出
- 金色熊的族群數量降至原本數量的三分之一，倍斯特島嶼的海洋動物減少了 68%，花朵的多樣性減少了 72%

23｜subdued / elevenfold / plateau

- 今年成長減緩，減弱的颶風仍舊令人畏懼，科技股的成長已經日益減緩
- 科技股有著 11 倍的增加，達到 2019 年的 12 億元，水的溫度有顯著的暖化、11 倍的增長，足球隊能夠獲取 11 倍的獎酬
- 出生率在 1960 時達到了高原期、野生老虎在復甦後卻有著顯著的下滑，掠食者都會遇到高原期階段

PART 2　雅思精選小作文範文

雅思百變
圖表題字彙

Unit 1

☆ 單元概述

　　這個單元中介紹了高階字彙 sag，表示「（物價等）下降」，在例句中更搭配了高階慣用語 is lumbered with，可以將此搭配也一併記起來，適時運用於作文中取代其他較常見的表達。第二個字彙介紹了常見的 account for，並搭配了整體利潤的占比、束帶蛇的出口和所占的水族館營運支出百分比。最後一個字彙則介紹了 stand at，也是高分的表達語，可以將這三個例句都記起來，用於股票等位於新高點或某個數值。

圖表題高分字彙 ▶ *MP3 001*

【1. sag（物價等）下降，下跌、萎靡】

- Fruit sales have tripled to 9 million dollars, but profits **sagged**.
水果的銷售已增長了三倍來到九百萬美元，但是利潤卻萎縮了。

Sag

【還能怎麼說】

- Best Clothing is lumbered with 5 million in outstanding debts, and its shares have also **sagged** to a new low, according to the news.
倍斯特服飾為 5 百萬的積欠款項所拖累，而其股票也已降至新低點，根據新聞所述。

- The owner of the Best Precious Stone announced recently that miscalculations at the **sagging** archaeological site had cost 5 billion financial losses, equivalent to all investors' money.
倍斯特稀有寶石近期宣布錯誤估算價值正下跌的考古遺址已經導致了 50 億元的財政損失，同於所有投資客的錢。

23

Account for

【2. account for 佔...比例】

- The latest released game consoles will **account for** at least 35% of the overall profits in 2023.

  最新發佈的遊戲主機將會至少佔有 2023 年整體利潤的百分之三十五。

【還能怎麼說】

- Best Circus previously **accounted for** 67% of garter snake exports, but a rival company has come up with an undercutting strategy.

  倍斯特馬戲團早先占有束帶蛇百分之六十七的出口，但其競爭對手已想出了削價競爭的策略。

- Green fluorescent ribbon snakes will generate 6 billion in economic output, **accounting for** 78% of Best Aquarium's operating expenditures.

  綠色螢光襪帶蛇將產出 60 億元的經濟產量，占倍斯特水族館營運支出的百分之七十八。

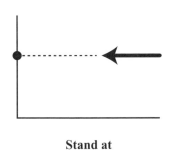

Stand at

【3. stand at（身高，溫度，得分等）是……[（+at）]】

■ During the fiscal year, Best Automobile's overseas profits peaked at 70 million dollars, whereas its rival **stood at** 1 billion.
在財政年度期間，倍斯特汽車的海外利潤達到 7 千萬元的高峰，而其競爭對手的利潤卻是 10 億元。

【還能怎麼說】

■ Best Automobile's flatlining profits **stood at** 5 million dollars, and foreign investors has not shown the slightest interest in the languishing firm.
倍斯特汽車維持靜止不動的利潤為 5 百萬元，而國外投資客對這樣疲軟無力的公司毫無興致。

■ By the time the CEO of the Best Circus accepted the job at another lucrative firm, he had already sold 25% shares of the Best Circus, the share which **stood at** a new high of 75.9.
在倍斯特馬戲團的執行長接受另一間賺大錢公司的工作時，他已經售出倍斯特馬戲團百分之二十五的股票，該股票位於新高點 75.9。

❶ 倍斯特服飾為 5 百萬的積欠款項所拖累,而其股票也已降至新低點,根據新聞所述。

_____

_____

【參考答案】

Best Clothing is lumbered with 5 million in outstanding debts, and its shares have also sagged to a new low, according to the news.

❷ 倍斯特稀有寶石近期宣布錯誤估算價值正下跌的考古遺址已經導致了 50 億元的財政損失,同於所有投資客的錢。

_____

_____

【參考答案】

The owner of the Best Precious Stone announced recently that miscalculations at the sagging archaeological site had cost 5 billion financial losses, equivalent to all investors' money.

❸ 綠色螢光襪帶蛇將產出 60 億元的經濟產量,占倍斯特水族館營運支出的百分之七十八。

_____

_____

雅思精選小作文範文

【參考答案】
Green fluorescent ribbon snakes will generate 6 billion in economic output, accounting for 78% of Best Aquarium's operating expenditures.

❹ 倍斯特汽車維持靜止不動的利潤為 5 百萬元，而國外投資客對這樣疲軟無力的公司毫無興致。

_____

_____

【參考答案】
Best Automobile's flatlining profits stood at 5 million dollars, and foreign investors has not shown the slightest interest in the languishing firm.

❺ 在倍斯特馬戲團的執行長接受另一間賺大錢公司的工作時，他已經售出倍斯特馬戲團百分之二十五的股票，該股票位於新高點 75.9。

_____

_____

【參考答案】
By the time the CEO of the Best Circus accepted the job at another lucrative firm, he had already sold 25% shares of the Best Circus, the share which stood at a new high of 75.9.

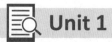

Questions 1-14 Complete the summary

Fruit sales have tripled to 9 million dollars, but profits **1.** _____ _____.

Best Clothing is **2.** _____ with 5 million in **3.** _____ debts, and its shares have also sagged to a new low, according to the news.

The owner of the Best Precious Stone announced recently that **4.** _____ at the sagging archaeological site had cost 5 billion financial losses, equivalent to all investors' money.

The latest released game **5.** _____ will account for at least 35% of the overall profits in 2023.

Best Circus previously **6.** _____ 67% of garter snake exports, but a rival company has come up with an **7.** _____ strategy.

Green **8.** _____ ribbon snakes will generate 6 billion in economic output, accounting for 78% of Best Aquarium's operating **9.** _____.

During the fiscal year, Best Automobile's overseas profits **10.** _____ at 70 million dollars, whereas its rival stood at 1 billion.

Best Automobile's **11.** _____ profits stood at 5 million dollars, and foreign investors has not shown the slightest interest in the **12.** _____ firm.

By the time the CEO of the Best Circus accepted the job at another **13.** _____ firm, he had already sold 25% **14.** _____ of the Best Circus, the share which stood at a new high of 75.9.

Boxes

A accounted for	**B** consoles
C fluorescent	**D** undercutting
E peaked	**F** languishing
G lumbered	**H** outstanding
I flatlining	**J** miscalculations
K sagged	**L** lucrative
M shares	**N** expenditures

參考答案

1. K	2. G	3. H	4. J	5. B	6. A	7. D
8. C	9. N	10. E	11. I	12. F	13. L	14. M

雅思百變
圖表題字彙

Unit 2

★ 單元概述

　　這個單元中介紹了高階字彙 hover，可以用於表達某個數值或股價等的徘徊，提升字彙表達力，跟股市的搭配表達，如果不熟的話，可以參照例句。拋售和交易量等字彙也可以一併學起來。第二個介紹的字是形容詞但也至關重要，whooping 的使用遠比其他的同義字更有力，且容易獲得高的評價。例句中搭配花青素的例句和 compared with 的連用部分可以背起來用於比較圖表題的數值。最後一個字很常見，不過可以順道記憶搭配百分比的用法和搭配銷售數值的表達，更靈活的運用這個單字。

圖表題高分字彙 ▶ MP3 002

【4. hover 徘徊；停留】

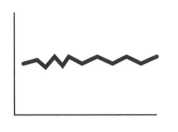

Hover

- Best Precious Stone's gold stocks **hovered** around US 30.5-31 in the early morning, up 5% from yesterday's trading.

  在稍早的早晨，倍斯特珍貴寶石的黃金股價徘徊在約 30.5 至 31 美元，從昨天的交易量上漲了 5%。

【還能怎麼說】

- Based on data from about 100 investors, analysts have found that their investment **hovers** around US 50,000-50,500 per month.

  根據大約 100 位投資客的資料，分析師已經發現了他們的投資徘徊在每個月 5 萬美元至 5 萬 500 美元間。

- Investors who have been familiar with stock markets are much better at identifying stocks that **hover** around a certain figure a sign to undersell.

  對於股票市場一直以來都很熟稔的投資客更擅長於辨識出徘徊在特定數值的股票是拋售的徵兆。

【5. whopping 巨大的；異常的】

Whopping

- Compared with rare fruits' **whopping** quantity of anthocyanin, strawberry's anthocyanin per 100g contains far less.

比起稀有水果巨額的花青素含量，草莓每 100 公克所含有的花青素量更為稀少。

....

【還能怎麼說】

- Researchers found a higher than normal, **whopping** level of toxin in golden snakes' blood vessels.

研究人員們在金蛇血管內發現了高於正常水平、異常大量的毒素。

- Without effective control methods, **whopping** surges of harmful chemicals in marine mammals are bound to happen in the near future.

缺乏有效的控制方法，在海洋哺乳類動物體內異常激增的有害化學物質，在未來一定會發生。

....

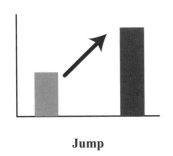

Jump

【6. jump 攀升】

- In its second day of trading, sales figures **jumped** 20% to 40 NT dollars.

  在第二天的交易，銷售數值攀升 20% 來到新台幣 40 元。

【還能怎麼說】

- The increased transmissibility of malaria **jumped** 50% due to a new variant.

  由於新的變異株，瘧疾傳染性的增強攀升至百分之五十。

- So far, only 5 cases of tigers' accidental death have been found in the region, but wildlife biologists are worried that the number will **jump** to at least 50% in the peak season of tourism.

  到目前為止，僅有 5 例的老虎意外死亡在該地區被發現，但是野生生物學家們擔心，意外死亡的數量在旅遊觀光旺季時會攀升到至少百分之五十。

❶ 在稍早的早晨，倍斯特珍貴寶石的黃金股價徘迴在約 30.5 至 31 美元，從昨天的交易量上漲了 5%。

_____

_____

【參考答案】

Best Precious Stone's gold stocks hovered around US 30.5-31 in the early morning, up 5% from yesterday's trading.

❷ 對於股票市場一直以來都很熟稔的投資客更擅長於辨識出徘徊在特定數值的股票是拋售的徵兆。

_____

_____

【參考答案】

Investors who have been familiar with stock markets are much better at identifying stocks that hover around a certain figure a sign to undersell.

❸ 比起稀有水果巨額的花青素含量，草莓每 100 公克所含有的花青素量更為稀少。

_____

_____

【參考答案】

Compared with rare fruits' whopping quantity of anthocyanin, strawberry's anthocyanin per 100g contains far less.

❹ 由於新的變異株，瘧疾傳染性的增強攀升至百分之五十。

_____

_____

【參考答案】

The increased transmissibility of malaria jumped 50% due to a new variant.

❺ 到目前為止，僅有 5 例的老虎意外死亡在該地區被發現，但是野生生物學家們擔心，意外死亡的數量在旅遊觀光旺季時會攀升到至少百分之五十。

_____

_____

【參考答案】

So far, only 5 cases of tigers' accidental death have been found in the region, but wildlife biologists are worried that the number will jump to at least 50% in the peak season of tourism.

 **Unit 2**

Questions 1-14 Complete the summary

Best Precious Stone's gold stocks **1.** _____ around US 30.5-31 in the early morning, up 5% from yesterday's trading.

Based on data from about 100 investors, analysts have found that their **2.** _____ hovers around US 50,000-50,500 per month.

Investors who have been familiar with stock markets are much better at **3.** _____ stocks that hover around a certain figure a sign to undersell.

Compared with rare fruits' **4.** _____ quantity of anthocyanin, strawberry's anthocyanin per 100g **5.** _____ __ far less.

Researchers found a higher than normal, whopping level of **6.** _____ in golden snakes' blood **7.** _____.

Without **8.** _____ control methods, whopping **9.** _____ _____ of harmful chemicals in marine mammals are bound to happen in the near future.

In its second day of trading, sales **10.** _____ jumped 20% to 40 NT dollars.

The increased **11.** _____ of malaria jumped 50% due to a new **12.** _____.

So far, only 5 cases of tigers' **13.** _____ death have been found in the region, but wildlife biologists are worried that the number will jump to at least 50% in the peak season of **14.** _____.

Boxes

A transmissibility		**B** contains
C accidental		**D** variant
E figures		**F** tourism
G investment		**H** identifying
I effective		**J** toxin
K surges		**L** whopping
M hovered		**N** vessels

參考答案

1. M	2. G	3. H	4. L	5. B	6. J	7. N
8. I	9. K	10. E	11. A	12. D	13. C	14. F

雅思百變
圖表題字彙

Unit 3

★ 單元概述

　　這個單元中介紹了高階字彙 command，在前一個單元中有介紹了 account for，如果遇到像是圓餅圖就很適合使用這兩個字和片語接續表達，而非將 account for 用於表達占比的部分從頭用到尾。當中有搭配股份的部分，可以參考例句的使用。

　　第二個字彙介紹了高分字彙 escalation，建議多使用 escalation 並減少使用 increase，讓考官知道你也會這個字。在大多數的作文中，許多考生將 increase 或 decrease 用了太多次，不利於獲取更高的作文分數。例句中搭配了價格和產量使用，可以把用法都記起來。最後介紹了一個高階片語，但在英語雜誌或報導中也很常見，建議把它背起來，絕對是獲取 8 分以上的關鍵高階片語，使用時還是要特別注意當中的時態等，以免被扣分。

圖表題高分字彙 ▶ *MP3 003*

Command

【7. command 握有】

■ In 2020, Best Automobile **commanded** 51% of the subsidiary of Asia's Apparel, implying that it had the total control of the clothing giant.
在 2020 年，倍斯特汽車握有百分之五十一的亞洲衣飾子公司的股權，意謂著它擁有這間服飾巨頭的全部控制權。

【還能怎麼說】

■ Best Circus will **command** 88% shares of ABC Zoo next month, so there is little hope for other investors to buy out shares from Best Circus and be a sole owner of the Zoo.
倍斯特馬戲團將於下個月時握有百分之八十八的 ABC 動物園股份，所以其他投資客要從倍斯特馬戲團手上購回股份和當動物園的唯一持有人的機會是渺茫的。

■ Despite the fact that Best Technology **commands** 80% shares of other software giants, the double agent secretly gets confidential documents inside the building.
儘管倍斯特科技握有百分之八十其他軟體巨頭的股份，雙面特務秘密地從內部大樓中獲取了機密的文件。

39

Escalation

【8. escalation 上漲；增加】

■ Due to the recent **escalation** in vegetable prices, most restaurants have decided to reduce ingredients, such as tomatoes, in the dish.

由於近期蔬菜價格的上漲，大多數餐館已經決定要在菜餚中減少像是番茄的佐料。

【還能怎麼說】

■ Meanwhile, other countries are trying to control the **escalation** in food prices for fear that there will be a protest on the street.

與此同時，其他國家正試圖控制食物價格的上漲，唯恐在街上將有抗議出現。

■ Due to an **escalation** of tulip yields in the local area, flower shop owners suspended some overseas shipments.

由於當地鬱金香產量的增加，花店店主中止了一些海外的運輸。

【9. tick up 上漲；上升】

■ Despite the fact that revenue of rare aquamarine spiders **ticked up** 25% to US 600 dollars, investors still had concerns about the fluctuation of the prices in the past few weeks.

儘管稀有的海藍色蜘蛛的收益上漲了 25%來到 600 美元，投資客對於過去幾周價格的波動仍感到擔憂。

Tick up

【還能怎麼說】

■ The financial analysis report suggests that more advertising won't **tick up** the price, so companies have to think outside the box.

財政分析報告建議更多的廣告不會讓價格有所上升，所以公司必須要跳脫框架思考。

■ In September, food prices began **ticking up** unusually fast in suburb areas, making fruit farmers jubilant.

在九月，物價在郊區開始異常快速地上漲，讓水果農們興高采烈。

❶ 在 2020 年，倍斯特汽車握有百分之五十一的亞洲衣飾子公司的股權，意謂著它擁有這間服飾巨頭的全部控制權。

_____

_____

【參考答案】

In 2020, Best Automobile commanded 51% of the subsidiary of Asia's Apparel, implying that it had the total control of the clothing giant.

❷ 由於近期蔬菜價格的上漲，大多數餐館已經決定要在菜餚中減少像是番茄的佐料。

_____

_____

【參考答案】

Due to the recent escalation in vegetable prices, most restaurants have decided to reduce ingredients, such as tomatoes, in the dish.

❸ 由於當地鬱金香產量的增加，花店店主中止了一些海外的運輸。

_____

_____

【參考答案】

Due to an **escalation** of tulip yields in the local area, flower shop owners suspended some overseas shipments.

❹ 儘管稀有的海藍色蜘蛛的收益上漲了 25% 來到 600 美元，投資客對於過去幾周價格的波動仍感到擔憂。

_____

_____

【參考答案】

Despite the fact that revenue of rare aquamarine spiders ticked up 25% to US 600 dollars, investors still had concerns about the fluctuation of the prices in the past few weeks.

❺ 財政分析報告建議更多的廣告不會讓價格有所上升，所以公司必須要跳脫框架思考。

_____

_____

【參考答案】

The financial analysis report suggests that more advertising won't tick up the price, so companies have to think outside the box.

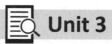

Questions 1-14 Complete the summary

In 2020, Best Automobile **1.** _____ 51% of the **2.** _____ _____ of Asia's Apparel, implying that it had the total control of the clothing giant.

Best Circus will command 88% shares of ABC Zoo next month, so there is little **3.** _____ for other investors to buy out shares from Best Circus and be a sole owner of the Zoo.

Despite the fact that Best Technology commands 80% shares of other **4.** _____ giants, the double agent secretly gets **5.** _____ documents inside the building.

Due to the recent **6.** _____ in vegetable prices, most restaurants have decided to **7.** _____ ingredients, such as tomatoes, in the dish.

Meanwhile, other countries are trying to **8.** _____ the escalation in food prices for fear that there will be a protest on the street.

Due to an escalation of tulip **9.** _____ in the local area, flower shop owners **10.** _____ some overseas shipments.

Despite the fact that revenue of rare **11.** _____ spiders ticked up 25% to US 600 dollars, investors still had concerns about the **12.** _____ of the prices in the past few weeks.

The financial analysis report suggests that more **13.** _____ ____ won't tick up the price, so companies have to think outside the box.

In September, food prices began ticking up unusually fast in suburb areas, making fruit farmers **14.** _____.

Boxes

A fluctuation	**B** software
C control	**D** escalation
E commanded	**F** subsidiary
G jubilant	**H** confidential
I reduce	**J** yields
K aquamarine	**L** hope
M suspended	**N** advertising

參考答案

1. E	2. F	3. L	4. B	5. H	6. D	7. I
8. C	9. J	10. M	11. K	12. A	13. N	14. G

雅思百變
圖表題字彙

Unit 4

★ 單元概述

第一個字彙介紹了也是獲取 8 分以上的關鍵高階片語 rake in，在例句中分別有三個時態的搭配，包含過去式、現在完成式和動名詞當主詞的用法，如果有擔心時態的使用會被扣分的考生，可以參考例句中的表達。第二個字彙介紹了 expand，是個常見的字彙，如果能使用這類的動詞就盡量要使用上，以減少文句中的贅字。當中有搭配百分比和淨利率等的用法也可以快速記起來，並使用在圓餅圖等圖表中。最後介紹的片語 fall short of 則可以用於比較兩個圖表時使用，未達預期另一個隱晦的意思就是表示出兩個表格中年度中的差異部分。各數值相似或相異處都是考官看的重點。

 圖表題高分字彙 ▶ *MP3 004*

【10. rake in 迅速（或大量）取得（錢財等）[（+in）]】

■ At the same time, Best Circus **raked in** 5.5 million dollars in operating revenue, a sharp increase from last year.

與此同時，倍斯特馬戲團迅速取得了 550 萬元的公司營運收入，比起去年有急遽的增長。

Rake in

【還能怎麼說】

■ More than 17 months into adventures, 65% of the adventurers have **raked in** a significant amount of gold that will be enough for three generations to use.

超過 17 個月的冒險，百分之六十五的冒險家們迅速取得了顯著的黃金量，足夠三代使用。

■ **Raking in** a great deal of money may seem likely in the mythology-like maze, but there is still a great chance that you will get injured during the journey.

迅速獲取大量的錢可能在神話般的迷宮內是可能的，但是仍有很大的機會是，你在途中受到傷害。

【 11. expand 擴大；增加 】

Expand

■ Best Clothing has been anticipating a rise in orders from other manufacturers so that the net profit can **expand** 20% from 2021 to 10 billion in 2023.

倍斯特服飾一直都期待從其他製造商那裡獲取更多訂單數，這樣一來公司的淨收益就能比起 2021 年時擴增百分之二十，來到 2023 年的 100 億元。

【 還能怎麼說 】

■ Best Cinema has been hoping to **expand** its profit margins to at least 15% by creating a platform.

倍斯特影視一直希望藉由創造一個平台擴增至少百分之十五的淨利率。

■ The black market **expanded** 65% due to an increasing demand in desert gems and precious herbs.

黑市擴增了百分之六十五，由於在沙漠寶石和珍貴藥草有日益增加的需求。

【 12. fall short of 低於預期；未達到 】

■ Customers visiting the site has experienced a surge, but the expected goal has obviously **fallen short of** 50 million dollars, according to the report.

參訪該位址的消費者已經激增，但是顯然未達到預期的 5 千萬元，根據報導。

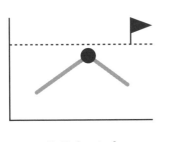

Fall short of

【 還能怎麼說 】

■ Diamonds continues to be infrequent in many regions, so extracting them for profits only makes the goal **fallen short of** the company's goal.

鑽石在許多地區始終很罕見，掘取鑽石獲利只是讓這個目標低於公司預期。

■ The performance is still **falling short of** the target given by the high-ups, so the circus animal will probably get inhumane treatment.

表現仍未達到高層所給予的目標，所以馬戲團的動物將可能會受到不人道的對待。

❶ 與此同時，倍斯特馬戲團迅速取得了 550 萬元的公司營運收入，比起去年有急遽的增長。

_____

_____

【參考答案】

At the same time, Best Circus raked in 5.5 million dollars in operating revenue, a sharp increase from last year.

❷ 倍斯特服飾一直都期待從其他製造商那裡獲取更多訂單數，這樣一來公司的淨收益就能比起 2021 年時擴增百分之二十，來到 2023 年的 100 億元。

_____

_____

【參考答案】

Best Clothing has been anticipating a rise in orders from other manufacturers so that the net profit can expand 20% from 2021 to 10 billion in 2023.

❸ 倍斯特影視一直希望藉由創造一個平台擴增至少百分之十五的淨利率。

_____

_____

【參考答案】

Best Cinema has been hoping to expand its profit margins to at least 15% by creating a platform.

❹ 鑽石在許多地區始終很罕見，掘取鑽石獲利只是讓這個目標低於公司預期。

_____

_____

【參考答案】

Diamonds continues to be infrequent in many regions, so extracting them for profits only makes the goal fallen short of the company's goal.

❺ 表現仍未達到高層所給予的目標，所以馬戲團的動物將可能會受到不人道的對待。

_____

_____

【參考答案】

The performance is still falling short of the target given by the high-ups, so the circus animal will probably get inhumane treatment.

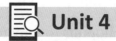

Questions 1-14 Complete the summary

At the same time, Best Circus **1.** _____ 5.5 million dollars in operating revenue, a sharp increase from last year.

More than 17 months into **2.** _____, 65% of the adventurers have raked in a significant amount of gold that will be enough for three generations to use.

3. _____ a great deal of money may seem likely in the mythology-like maze, but there is still a great chance that you will get injured during the journey.

Best Clothing has been **4.** _____ a rise in orders from other manufacturers so that the net profit can **5.** _____ __ 20% from 2021 to 10 billion in 2023.

Best Cinema has been hoping to expand its profit margins to at least 15% by creating a **6.** _____.

The **7.** _____ market expanded 65% due to an increasing demand in **8.** _____ gems and precious herbs.

Customers visiting the site has experienced a **9.** _____, but the **10.** _____ goal has obviously fallen short of 50 million dollars, according to the report.

Diamonds continues to be **11.** _____ in many regions, so **12.** _____ them for profits only makes the goal fallen short of the company's goal.

The **13.** _____ is still falling short of the target given by the high-ups, so the circus animal will probably get **14.** _____ treatment.

Part 2

雅思精選小作文範文

Boxes

A infrequent

B expand

C surge

D platform

E expected

F black

G raking in

H desert

I performance

J adventures

K anticipating

L extracting

M raked in

N inhumane

參考答案

1. M	2. J	3. G	4. K	5. B	6. D	7. F
8. H	9. C	10. E	11. A	12. L	13. I	14. N

雅思百變
圖表題字彙

Unit 5

★ 單元概述

　　第一個字彙介紹了高階字彙 uptick，也能用於取代 increase，如果圖表題中有多處是表示增加的部分，可以跟先前的 escalation 替換呈現在各個文句中，避免都使用 increase。在例句中也有與高階形容詞像是 remarkable 等的搭配，可以學起來並運用在作文中。另外介紹了兩個字彙分別是 plunge 和 sink，這兩個字也能輪流使用，以避免重複，有時候可能在考試當下突然忘記可以至少用到 sink，但是也要注意時態，尤其 sink 的三態變化。

圖表題高分字彙 ▶ *MP3 005*

【13. uptick 數量的增長】

■ Best Cinema has seen a remarkable **uptick** in tickets sold in the past few weeks due to herd immunity in the area.
由於該地區的群體免疫，倍斯特影視在過去幾周的電影票銷售量有顯著的增加。

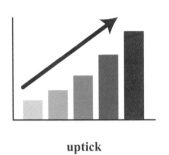
uptick

【還能怎麼說】

■ Bee stings caused by purple hornets in the fiction have been linked to an **uptick** in the number of people searching for the longevity.
在小說中，由紫色大黃蜂所引起的蜂螫已與找尋長壽人們數量的上升有所關連。

■ The mountain's verdant present is the main reason why there has been a noticeable **uptick** in the number of people visiting here.
山上出現翠綠如茵的景象是觀光此地人數一直有顯著增加的原因。

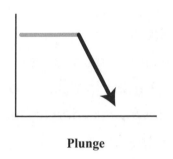

Plunge

【 14. plunge 下降，急降；猛跌 】

■ Visitor arrivals to Best Zoo **plunged** 50% in October, making investors increasingly worried.
到倍斯特動物園參訪的旅客在 10 月份急降了百分之五十，讓投資客與日俱增地感到擔憂。

【 還能怎麼說 】

■ Interviewees attending tech firms' interview **plunged** 70% because of the unreliable report that painted them as sweatshops.
參加科技公司面試的面試者急遽下降了百分之七十，因為不可靠的報導將它們描繪成血汗工廠。

■ The ratio of chip failures can be remedied, but changes in temperatures can still facilitate the high fault rate, **plunging** 70% of overall production.
晶片不合格的比率可以修復，但是溫度的變化仍可能促成高錯誤率，整體產出猛降百分之七十。

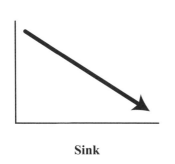

Sink

【15. sink 下降，降至】

■ High-yield bonds **sank** to minus 10.5% on Nov 25, the lowest record in 10 years.
在 11 月 25 日，高收益債卷降至負百分之十點五，是近十年來最低紀錄。

【還能怎麼說】

■ The ratio of chip faults **has sunk** to 5% thanks to a team of skillful and meticulous engineers working around the clock.
晶片的缺失比率已降至百分之五，多虧了熟練且小心翼翼的工程師們日以繼夜地工作著。

■ Fewer golden snakes will meander through this route because it will make their body temperatures **sink** too low to maintain normal metabolism.
較少數量的金蛇會蜿蜒穿過此路徑，因為這會讓牠們的體溫降得太低而無法維持正常的代謝。

57

❶ 在小說中，由紫色大黃蜂所引起的蜂螫已與找尋長壽人們數量的上升有所關連。

_____

_____

【參考答案】
Bee stings caused by purple hornets in the fiction have been linked to an uptick in the number of people searching for the longevity.

❷ 參加科技公司面試的面試者急遽下降了百分之七十，因為不可靠的報導將它們描繪成血汗工廠。

_____

_____

【參考答案】
Interviewees attending tech firms' interview plunged 70% because of the unreliable report that painted them as sweatshops.

❸ 晶片不合格的比率可以修復，但是溫度的變化仍可能促成高錯誤率。

_____

_____

【參考答案】

The ratio of chip failures can be remedied, but changes in temperatures can still facilitate the high fault rate.

❹ 在 11 月 25 日，高收益債卷降至負百分之十點五，是近十年來最低紀錄。

_____

_____

【參考答案】

High-yield bonds sank to minus 10.5% on Nov 25, the lowest record in 10 years.

❺ 晶片的缺失比率已降至百分之五，多虧了熟練且小心翼翼的工程師們日以繼夜地工作著。

_____

_____

【參考答案】

The ratio of chip faults has sunk to 5% thanks to a team of skillful and meticulous engineers working around the clock.

Questions 1-14 Complete the summary

Best Cinema has seen a remarkable **1.** _____ in tickets sold in the past few weeks due to herd immunity in the area.

Bee stings caused by **2.** _____ hornets in the fiction have been linked to an uptick in the number of people searching for the **3.** _____.

The mountain's **4.** _____ present is the main reason why there has been a **5.** _____ uptick in the number of people visiting here.

Visitor arrivals to Best Zoo **6.** _____ 50% in October, making investors increasingly worried.

Interviewees attending tech firms' interview plunged 70% because of the **7.** _____ report that painted them as **8.** _____.

The ratio of chip failures can be **9.** _____, but changes in temperatures can still **10.** _____ the high fault rate.

High-yield bonds sank to **11.** _____ 10.5% on Nov 25, the lowest record in 10 years.

The ratio of chip faults has sunk to 5% thanks to a team of skillful and meticulous **12.** _____ working around the clock.

Fewer golden snakes will **13.** _____ through this route because it will make their body temperatures sink too low to maintain normal **14.** _____.

Boxes

A minus

B engineers

C unreliable

D plunged

E meander

F metabolism

G purple

H noticeable

I sweatshops

J remedied

K longevity

L verdant

M uptick

N facilitate

參考答案

1. M	2. G	3. K	4. L	5. H	6. D	7. C
8. I	9. J	10. N	11. A	12. B	13. E	14. F

雅思百變圖表題字彙

Unit 6

★ 單元概述

　　第一個字彙介紹了 swell，表示「增加」，是當動詞的用法，也能取代許多其他較低階的字彙，其中的例句還搭配了先前介紹的 stand at，越是用到更多書中介紹的字彙在一個句子中，除了表達更好外，也越能獲取更佳的分數段。而 decline 的部分則是介紹了搭配了百分比的用法/當名詞的用法，也可以試著使用其當動詞的用法，能更靈活的表達，讀起來也會比死板的範文更為增色。最後一個字彙則介紹了 surpass，這三個例句都表達很細節且具體，也可以都背起來，當中還包含了範圍間的數值和搭配 jump 等字彙的使用，讓描繪出口量時更具體表達出當中的變化。

圖表題高分字彙 ▶ *MP3 006*

【16. swell 增長；增加】

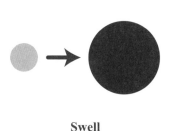

Swell

■ Best Bank's heavy liabilities stood at 5 billion dollars in August, and analysts were worried that they might **swell** to an amount that the bank could no longer afford.
在 8 月份，倍斯特銀行沉重的債務為 50 億元，而分析師擔憂，負債的金額會膨脹至銀行都無力負擔的情況。

【還能怎麼說】

■ The number of crimson dolphins will **swell** to 100 in a single day because they consume dragon meat, according to the fiction.
根據小說，暗紅色海豚的數量會於一日之間增加至 100 隻，因為牠們攝食龍肉。

■ Dragon meat will be used to **swell** warrior's muscle and resistant to water pressure, so it is considered pretty precious in the fiction.
龍肉會被用於增進戰士的肌肉和抗水壓能力，所以在小說中被視為是相當珍貴的。

63

Decline

【 17. decline 下降，下跌；減少 】

■ The sales of golden octopuses have dropped over the past few years in the black market, along with a 70% **decline** among treasure collectors.

金色章魚的銷售量已在過去幾年的黑市中有所下降，在賞金獵人中，價格也有百分之七十的下滑。

【 還能怎麼說 】

■ Snake bites caused by golden serpents from the mountain cliff have been linked to a **decline** in tourists in the area.

由山崖處的金色毒蛇所導致的毒蛇咬傷與這個地區觀光客數量減少一直有關聯。

■ Remains of exceedingly large octopuses have been found on several sites, but the number has had a **decline** due to rampant poaching activities.

異常巨大的章魚遺骸已在幾個地點發掘了，但是由於猖獗的盜獵活動使得數量減少了。

【18. surpass 勝過；優於；大於】

■ Consumption of strawberries grew 25% last year to US 20 dollars per basket, so local residents are predicting that the demand will **surpass** that rate this year, to perhaps 39%.

在去年，草莓的消費增長了 25%來到每籃 20 美元，所以當地居民預測需求會比起今年超出很多，可能來到 39%。

Surpass

【還能怎麼說】

■ The blue snake market has grown considerably in several regions because blue snake's luminous attributes can be rivalled with fireflies, or **surpass** them.

藍色蛇的市場在幾個地區有顯著地增長，因為藍色蛇發光的特性能與螢火蟲披敵甚至勝過牠們。

■ Macabre crimson spider exports jumped 65% from 2017 to roughly 650 kilos in 2018, **surpassing** species of the similar kind.

恐怖的深紅色蜘蛛的出口量從 2017 年約略 650 公斤在 2018 年攀升了百分之六十五，超越同類的品種。

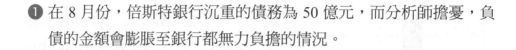

❶ 在 8 月份，倍斯特銀行沉重的債務為 50 億元，而分析師擔憂，負債的金額會膨脹至銀行都無力負擔的情況。

_____

_____

【參考答案】

Best Bank's heavy liabilities stood at 5 billion dollars in August, and analysts were worried that they might swell to an amount that the bank could no longer afford.

❷ 金色章魚的銷售量已在過去幾年的黑市中有所下降，在賞金獵人中，價格也有百分之七十的下滑。

_____

_____

【參考答案】

The sales of golden octopuses have dropped over the past few years in the black market, along with a 70% decline among treasure collectors.

❸ 異常巨大的章魚遺骸已在幾個地點發掘了，但是由於猖獗的盜獵活動使得數量減少了。

_____

_____

【參考答案】

Remains of exceedingly large octopuses have been found on several sites, but the number has had a decline due to rampant poaching activities.

❹ 在去年，草莓的消費增長了 25%來到每籃 20 美元，所以當地居民預測需求會比起今年超出很多，可能來到 39%。

【參考答案】

Consumption of strawberries grew 25% last year to US 20 dollars per basket, so local residents are predicting that the demand will **surpass** that rate this year, to perhaps 39%.

❺ 藍色蛇的市場在幾個地區有顯著地增長，因為藍色蛇發光的特性能與螢火蟲披敵甚至勝過牠們。

【參考答案】

The blue snake market has grown considerably in several regions because blue snake's luminous attributes can be rivalled with fireflies, or surpass them.

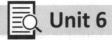 **Unit 6**

Questions 1-14 Complete the summary

Best Bank's heavy **1.** _____ stood at 5 billion dollars in August, and analysts were worried that they might swell to an amount that the bank could no longer afford.

The number of **2.** _____ dolphins will swell to 100 in a single day because they **3.** _____ dragon meat, according to the fiction.

Dragon meat will be used to swell warrior's muscle and **4.** _____ to water pressure, so it is considered pretty precious in the fiction.

The sales of golden octopuses have dropped over the past few years in the black market, along with a 70% **5.** _____ among treasure collectors.

Snake bites caused by golden **6.** _____ from the mountain cliff have been linked to a decline in tourists in the area.

Remains of **7.** _____ large octopuses have been found on several sites, but the number has had a decline due to rampant **8.** _____ activities.

9. _____ of strawberries grew 25% last year to US 20 dollars per basket, so local residents are predicting that the demand will **10.** _____ that rate this year, to perhaps 39%.

Part 1
雅思百變圖表題字彙

The blue snake market has grown **11.** _____ in several regions because blue snake's **12.** _____ attributes can be rivalled with fireflies, or surpass them.

13. _____ crimson spider exports jumped 65% from 2017 to roughly 650 kilos in 2018, surpassing species of the **14.** _____ kind.

Part 2
雅思精選小作文範文

Boxes

A surpass

B considerably

C liabilities

D luminous

E poaching

F macabre

G decline

H crimson

I consume

J similar

K resistant

L serpents

M exceedingly

N consumption

參考答案

1. C	2. H	3. I	4. K	5. G	6. L	7. M
8. E	9. N	10. A	11. B	12. D	13. F	14. J

雅思百變
圖表題字彙

Unit 7

★ 單元概述

　　第一個字彙介紹了 number 當動詞，也是個重要的單字，可以跟 total 等輪流用在不同句子間，表示一個具體的整體數值為何，是個很清楚明確的字彙。第二個字彙則介紹了 triple，也是個高分字彙，如果跟 number 做搭配的話，則能用於先描述一個數值變化增加了三倍，所以總數來到多少，這樣考官更清楚。Triple 在例句中的用法則用到了現在完成式和動名詞當主詞的部分。最後介紹的是 equivalent 表示「等同於…」，比使用 the same as 更為高階，也可以輪替使用。考生也可以試著將這個單元介紹的三個字彙都使用在同個例句中。

圖表題高分字彙　▶ MP3 007

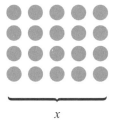

x

Number

【19. number 總數達到，共計】

■ The captain is now owning 60% of the lions on the island, **numbering** 360.

船長目前持有島上百分之六十的獅子數量，總計 360 頭。

【還能怎麼說】

■ High-tech industries have **numbered** 500 in the district, and it is estimated that the total will continue to grow.

在這個地區，高科技產業總數達到了 500 間，而估計總數量會持續成長。

■ Red fluorescent dragon eggs, **numbering** 4 in the dense forest, are exceedingly rare, and their glow will facilitate the flowering of golden orchids.

紅色螢光恐龍蛋在茂密的森林中的總數是 4 顆，相當罕見，而且牠們會促進金色蘭花的開花。

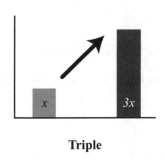

Triple

【 **20. triple** 增至三倍 】

- Thanks to abundance in rainfall this year, the yield of those desert berries has **tripled**.

  多虧今年豐沛的降雨，那些沙漠莓果的產量已經增加了三倍。

【 還能怎麼說 】

- Poachers trying to steal blue fluorescent dragon eggs have **tripled** to 90, but the shell of these eggs has been protected by an unknown chemical substance.

  試圖偷獵藍色螢光恐龍蛋的盜獵者數增加了三倍來到 90 人，但是這些恐龍蛋的外殼已經受到不明的化學物質所保護。

- **Tripling** the lure by offering more gold still cannot convince those local residents to steal purple fluorescent dragon eggs

  藉由提供更多的黃金，將誘因增至三倍仍無法讓那些當地居民信服到去偷取紫色螢光恐龍蛋。

【**21. equivalent** 相等的，等同於 [（+to）】】

■ Best Farm alone can generate apples that weigh almost 50 tons, **equivalent** to 20% of the global output.

倍斯特農場能夠獨自產出重達幾乎 50 噸的蘋果，等同於全球產量的百分之二十。

Equivalent

【還能怎麼說】

■ Warriors said that the sale of these golden apples in 1525 would increase by 90% from last year, making the price **equivalent** to the value of blue camels.

戰士們說道，在 1525 年，這些金蘋果的銷售會從去年度增加百分之九十，讓價格等同於藍色駱駝的價值。

■ Feeding these spiders with dragon meat will make them sizable, and they will be **equivalent** to the normal size of the pineapple.

以恐龍肉來餵食這些蜘蛛會讓牠們具有相當大的體型，而且牠們的體型會如同正常鳳梨大小。

❶ 紅色螢光恐龍蛋在茂密的森林中的總數是 4 顆,相當罕見,而且牠們會促進金色蘭花的開花。

_____

_____

【參考答案】

Red fluorescent dragon eggs, numbering 4 in the dense forest, are exceedingly rare, and their glow will facilitate the flowering of golden orchids.

❷ 試圖偷獵藍色螢光恐龍蛋的盜獵者數增加了三倍來到 90 人,但是這些恐龍蛋的外殼已經受到不明的化學物質所保護。

_____

_____

【參考答案】

Poachers trying to steal blue fluorescent dragon eggs have tripled to 90, but the shell of these eggs has been protected by an unknown chemical substance.

❸ 倍斯特農場能夠產出重達幾乎 50 噸的蘋果,等同於全球產量的百分之二十。

_____

_____

【參考答案】

Best Farm along can generate apples that weigh almost 50 ton, equivalent to 20% of the global output.

❹ 戰士們說道，在 1525 年，這些金蘋果的銷售會從去年度增加百分之九十，讓價格等同於藍色駱駝的價值。

_____

_____

【參考答案】

Warriors said that the sale of these golden apples in 1525 would increase by 90% from last year, making the price equivalent to the value of blue camels.

❺ 以恐龍肉來餵食這些蜘蛛會讓牠們具有相當大的體型，而且牠們的體型會如同正常鳳梨大小。

_____

_____

【參考答案】

Feeding these spiders with dragon meat will make them sizable, and they will be equivalent to the normal size of the pineapple.

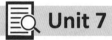

Questions 1-14 Complete the summary

The captain is now owning 60% of the lions on the island, **1.** __
_____ 360.

2. _____ industries have numbered 500 in the district,
and it is estimated that the total will continue to grow.

Red fluorescent dragon eggs, numbering 4 in the dense forest,
are exceedingly **3.** _____, and their glow will facilitate
the flowering of golden **4.** _____.

Thanks to **5.** _____ in rainfall this year, the yield of
those desert berries has tripled.

Poachers trying to **6.** _____ blue fluorescent dragon
eggs have tripled to 90, but the shell of these eggs has been
protected by an **7.** _____ chemical substance.

Tripling the **8.** _____ by offering more gold still cannot
convince those local **9.** _____ to steal purple
fluorescent dragon eggs

Best Farm alone can **10.** _____ apples that weigh
almost 50 tons, equivalent to 20% of the **11.** _____
output.

Warriors said that the sale of these golden apples in 1525
would **12.** _____ by 90% from last year, making the
price **13.** _____ to the value of blue camels.

Feeding these spiders with dragon meat will make them **14.** __
_____, and they will be equivalent to the normal size of
the pineapple.

Boxes

A numbering	**B** increase
C unknown	**D** sizable
E generate	**F** global
G lure	**H** equivalent
I high-tech	**J** residents
K steal	**L** abundance
M rare	**N** orchids

參考答案

1. A	2. I	3. M	4. N	5. L	6. K	7. C
8. G	9. J	10. E	11. F	12. B	13. H	14. D

雅思百變圖表題字彙

Unit 8

★ 單元概述

　　第一個字彙介紹了 shrink 是個高階的表達用語，更能減少考生慣用的 reduce 或 decrease 等字彙，是個更脫穎而出的字彙。在例句中還包含了搭配百分比的部分，以及股價平均減少了某個數值和在另一個句型中的變化，建議將這三個例句都記起來。第二個字彙介紹了 dip，也是個不錯的字彙，是個考生較少使用上的字彙，可以跟之前介紹的 sink 或 plunge 等輪替使用，在使用上也要注意時態的部分。Massive 是個常見的字彙，能用於修飾名詞，讓表達更為具體，表示數值變化是顯著的，還能用 immense，都比用 sharp increase 等更增色。

圖表題高分字彙 ▶ *MP3 008*

【**22. shrink** 縮小; 減少; 萎縮】

■ In 1990, the population of desert snakes **shrank** by 25% due to the weather condition, but it experienced a surge in the population after that.

由於天候因素，在 1990 年，沙漠蛇的族群數量萎縮了百分之二十五，但在那之後族群數卻有了激增。

【還能怎麼說】

■ According to the financial analysis, which examined the stock prices of Best Animal, shares **shrank** an average of 25% of their value after the rumor.

根據檢視倍斯特動物股價的金融分析，在謠言過後，股票價值會平均減至百分之二十五。

■ To make the size of these golden dragons **shrank**, magicians have been feeding them bee larvae and panda livers.

為了讓這些金色恐龍的體態縮小，魔術師一直餵食牠們蜜蜂幼蟲和熊貓肝臟。

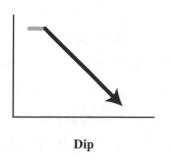

Dip

【23. dip 下沉，下降】

■ Piranhas have become increasingly rampant in the river, making the profit **dip** during the peak season of tourism.

在河裡，食人魚已變得日益猖獗，讓旅遊業的觀光旺季期的利潤下滑。

【還能怎麼說】

■ By introducing a great deal of marine dragons, the number of piranhas has **dipped** to a new low, making biologists pleased.

藉由引進大量的海洋恐龍，食人魚的數量已經降至新低點，讓生物學家們滿意。

■ The fierce blue dragon's dwelling was made more luxurious and spacious so that its number will not **dip**.

這個兇猛的藍色恐龍的居住地建造得更為豪華且寬敞，所以牠們的數量不會下降。

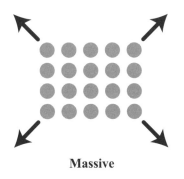

Massive

【**24. massive** 巨大的，大量的，大規模的】

■ A conclusion can be drawn about the **massive** drop in animal skin sales.

可以得出的結論為在動物皮的銷售中有大規模的減少。

【還能怎麼說】

■ 89% of red arctic dragon's dwelling seems to have been **massive** so that it will not affect its metabolism.

百分之八十九的紅色北極恐龍的居住地似乎是巨大的，這樣一來才不會影響牠們的代謝。

■ **Massive** rainfall in the area will influence the hatching of these green dragon eggs, so they have to be moved to a drier district.

這個地區大量的降雨將會影響這些綠色恐龍蛋的孵化，所以牠們必須要移到更為乾燥的地區。

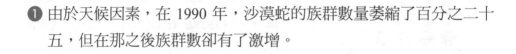

❶ 由於天候因素，在 1990 年，沙漠蛇的族群數量萎縮了百分之二十
五，但在那之後族群數卻有了激增。

_____

_____

【參考答案】

In 1990, the population of desert snakes shrank by 25% due to the
weather condition, but it experienced a surge in the population
after that.

❷ 根據檢視倍斯特動物股價的金融分析，在謠言過後，股票價值會
平均減至百分之二十五。

_____

_____

【參考答案】

According to the financial analysis, which examined the stock
prices of Best Animal, shares shrank an average of 25% of their
value after the rumor.

❸ 在河裡，食人魚已變得日益猖獗，讓旅遊業的觀光旺季期的利潤
下滑。

_____

_____

【參考答案】

Piranhas have become increasingly rampant in the river, making the profit dip during the peak season of tourism.

❹ 這個兇猛的藍色恐龍的居住地建造得更為豪華且寬敞,所以牠們的數量不會下降。

_____

_____

【參考答案】

The fierce blue dragon's dwelling was made more luxurious and spacious so that its number will not dip.

❺ 百分之八十九的紅色北極恐龍的居住地似乎是巨大的,這樣一來才不會影響牠們的代謝。

_____

_____

【參考答案】

89% of red arctic dragon's dwelling seems to have been massive so that it will not affect its metabolism.

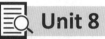

Questions 1-14 Complete the summary

In 1990, the population of desert snakes **1.** _____ by 25% due to the weather condition, but it experienced a surge in the population after that.

According to the financial analysis, which **2.** _____ the stock prices of Best Animal, shares shrank an **3.** _____ of 25% of their value after the rumor.

To make the size of these golden dragons shrank, **4.** _____ have been feeding them bee **5.** _____ and panda livers.

Piranhas have become increasingly **6.** _____ in the river, making the profit **7.** _____ during the peak season of tourism.

By **8.** _____ a great deal of marine dragons, the number of piranhas has dipped to a new low, making biologists pleased.

The fierce blue dragon's **9.** _____ was made more luxurious and spacious so that its number will not dip.

A conclusion can be drawn about the **10.** _____ drop in animal skin sales.

89% of red **11.** _____ dragon's dwelling seems to have been massive so that it will not affect its **12.** _____.

Massive rainfall in the area will influence the **13.** _____ of these green dragon eggs, so they have to be moved to a **14.** _____ district.

Boxes

A larvae	**B** examined
C rampant	**D** shrank
E introducing	**F** dwelling
G arctic	**H** dip
I metabolism	**J** massive
K drier	**L** hatching
M average	**N** magicians

參考答案

1. D	2. B	3. M	4. N	5. A	6. C	7. H
8. E	9. F	10. J	11. G	12. I	13. L	14. K

雅思百變
圖表題字彙

Unit 9

★ 單元概述

　　第一個字彙介紹了高階動詞 spike，例句中包含了動詞和名詞的用法，並搭配了失業率、貨物價格和關稅增加等，建議三個例句都背起來。Spike 也很適合用於曲線圖。第二個字彙介紹的是 decrease，很常見的用字，當中也包含了名詞和動詞的用法，也可以將例句再細節化，讓作文更添幾分色彩。最後一個介紹的是高分字彙 slump，前面有說過可以多用關鍵動詞就可以更簡潔表達出語意，slump 用於表達銳減，指大幅度的下滑等等，就可以省去副詞+表減少的動詞的搭配，而單獨使用 slump，例句中搭配了物種數量的銳減、股票的崩跌和水果產量的大幅減少，建議例句都背起來。

圖表題高分字彙　▶ MP3 009

【25. spike（通常指在下跌前）上升至非常高的數量（價格或程度）】

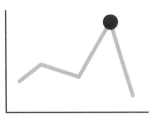

Spike

■ Due to the spread of the covid-19, economists are predicting that the unemployment rate will **spike** to 15.6%, terrifying most job seekers.

由於新冠疫情的傳播，經濟學家們預測失業率一定會升至百分之十五點六的幅度，震驚大多數的求職者。

【還能怎麼說】

■ The government concurred with enhancement of imports of Best Aquarium's goods and that led to a **spike** in the price.

政府同意提高倍斯特水族館的貨物進口，而那樣導致了價格的攀升。

■ The government had a **spike** in its tariffs on interdicted Best Aquarium's products to 55%, from 12%.

政府對於受制裁的倍斯特水族館的產品提高了關稅，從原先的百分之十二增加到百分之五十五。

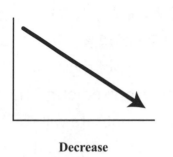

Decrease

【26. decrease 減；減少】

■ In July, the population of octopuses **decreased** 24% in value because of a surge of squids getting washed by the ocean current to the shore.

七月時，由於海洋洋流所沖到岸邊的烏魚數量的激增，章魚的族群數量的價值減少了百分之二十四。

【還能怎麼說】

■ A **decrease** in human birth rates is attributable to the touch of blue dragon's blood, and no cure has been found.

人類出生率的下滑歸咎於接觸到藍色恐龍的血液，且目前還沒有找到治療方法。

■ Drinking a bottle of yellow Antarctic dragon's blood will make people immune from any virus, **decreasing** harmful substances in blood vessels.

飲用一罐南極恐龍的血液會讓人們免疫於任何的病毒，降低血管裡的有害物質。

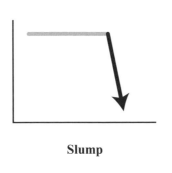

Slump

【**27. slump** 猛跌；滑坡；銳減】

- In 2000, growth of chameleons **slumped** to 50% in the region due to the increasing number of zebra snakes introduced in the area.

  在 2000 年，該地區變色龍數量的成長銳減了 50%，由於該地區所引進的日益增多的斑馬蛇。

【還能怎麼說】

- The CEO of Best Zoo has total assets estimated at 2 billion, but after the stock market crash on Tuesday morning, the stocks **slumped** to a new low.

  倍斯特動物園的總資產估算為 20 億元，但是在周二早晨的股市崩盤後，股票降到新低點。

- The yield of golden watermelons **slumped** to 50 kilos, so fruit farmers are hoping that the government will pour in emergent funds to save agriculture industries.

  金色西瓜的產量銳減至 50 公斤，所以果農希望政府能夠注入緊急資金以拯救農產業。

❶ 由於新冠疫情的傳播，經濟學家們預測失業率一定會升至百分之
十五點六的幅度，震驚大多數的求職者。

_____

_____

【參考答案】

Due to the spread of the covid-19, economists are predicting that
the unemployment rate will spike to 15.6%, terrifying most job
seekers.

❷ 政府對於受制裁的倍斯特水族館的產品提高了關稅，從原先的百
分之十二增加到百分之五十五。

_____

_____

【參考答案】

The government had a spike in its tariffs on interdicted Best
Aquarium's products to 55%, from 12%.

❸ 七月時，由於海洋洋流所沖到岸邊的烏魚數量的激增，章魚的族
群數量的價值減少了百分之二十四。

_____

_____

【參考答案】

In July, the population of octopuses decreased 24% in value because of a surge of squids getting washed by the ocean current to the shore.

❹ 飲用一罐南極恐龍的血液會讓人們免疫於任何的病毒，降低血管裡的有害物質。

_____

_____

【參考答案】

Drinking a bottle of yellow Antarctic dragon's blood will make people immune from any virus, decreasing harmful substances in blood vessels.

❺ 在 2000 年，該地區變色龍數量的成長銳減了百分之五十，由於該地區所引進的日益增多的斑馬蛇。

_____

_____

【參考答案】

In 2000, growth of chameleons slumped to 50% in the region due to the increasing number of zebra snakes introduced in the area.

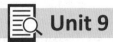 **Unit 9**

Questions 1-14 Complete the summary

Due to the spread of the covid-19, economists are predicting that the **1.** _____ rate will **2.** _____ to 15.6%, terrifying most job seekers.

The government concurred with **3.** _____ of imports of Best Aquarium's goods and that led to a spike in the price.

The government had a spike in its tariffs on **4.** _____ Best Aquarium's products to 55%, from 12%.

In July, the population of octopuses **5.** _____ 24% in value because of a surge of squids getting washed by the ocean **6.** _____ to the shore.

A decrease in human birth rates is **7.** _____ to the touch of blue dragon's blood, and no **8.** _____ has been found.

Drinking a bottle of yellow Antarctic dragon's blood will make people immune from any **9.** _____, decreasing harmful substances in blood **10.** _____.

In 2000, growth of chameleons **11.** _____ to 50% in the region due to the increasing number of zebra snakes **12.** __ _____ in the area.

The CEO of Best Zoo has total assets **13.** _____ at 2 billion, but after the stock market crash on Tuesday morning, the stocks slumped to a new low.

The yield of golden watermelons slumped to 50 kilos, so fruit farmers are hoping that the government will pour in **14.** _____ _____ funds to save agriculture industries.

Boxes

A enhancement	**B** unemployment
C virus	**D** interdicted
E decreased	**F** current
G vessels	**H** spike
I attributable	**J** cure
K estimated	**L** introduced
M emergent	**N** slumped

參考答案

1. B	2. H	3. A	4. D	5. E	6. F	7. I
8. J	9. C	10. G	11. N	12. L	13. K	14. M

雅思百變
圖表題字彙

Unit 10

⭐ 單元概述

　　第一個介紹了高分字彙 bulge，這個也是能迅速脫穎而出的單字，較少考生會用到這個字彙，其像是 increase 這類的名詞用法，所以不難用於句型中，但表示的是暫時的激增，搭配很廣泛，可以用於曲線圖中族群數量暫時的增長，之後數值可能又會有顯著的下滑。再來介紹的是 abating，搭配像是 show no sign…等就很好造句，考生可以試著使用當動詞時的用法或搭配現在完成進行式，用於表達出一直以來的減幅。最後介紹的是 dominate 表示占比，可以跟前面學到的 command 和 account for 接替使用，增添變化，但是其又代表了主要占的幅度，所以會像第一句的例句中的表達那樣。這句例句接續表達出所占的比例和次要的項目占比等的敘述手法，在圓餅圖等的表達中很司空見慣，還會搭配 followed by 等，不太算是高階的句型。

圖表題高分字彙 ▶ MP3 010

【28. bulge 暫時的激增；突然上漲】

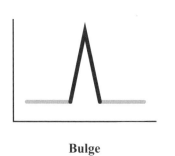

Bulge

- There was a **bulge** in the number of lions in July, but without perennial food sources, the number is back to the normal.

  在七月，獅子數量突然增加，但是缺乏永續不斷的食物來源，數量又回到正常水平。

【還能怎麼說】

- As can be seen from the graph, the growth of the health care stock had a **bulge** in 2019.

  如圖所示，在 2019 年，健康照護股票的成長有暫時的激增。

- Intrigued by the **bulge** in the number of tigers in August, scientists have decided to stay there for a couple of months.

  在八月時，老虎數量暫時激增，使得科學家們興致勃勃地決定要待在這裡幾個月。

95

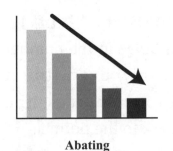

Abating

【**29. abating** 正減少；減弱；減輕；減退】

■ Losses are estimated at 5 billion dollars for the sugar plantations alone, and it shows no signs of **abating**.

僅是糖種植園的損失就預估來到 50 億元，且沒有減少的跡象。

【還能怎麼說】

■ Some nations suggested that the price of these fossil records be pegged down because they show no signs of **abating**.

有些國家建議要限制這些化石紀錄的價格，因為沒有跡象顯示它們會下跌。

■ The fiscal deficit of the desert village is estimated at 5 million dollars, and it shows no signs of **abating**.

這個沙漠村莊的財政赤字估計有 5 百萬元，且沒有減少的跡象。

【30. dominated 在⋯中占首要地位；擁有優勢；最明顯的】

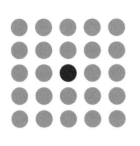

Dominated

- Of octopuses' diet in last summer, Pacific larger shrimps still **dominated** at 55%, followed by giant lobsters at 25% and crimson clams at 20%.

  在去年章魚的飲食中，太平洋蝦子仍舊佔據百分之五十五，接續是巨型龍蝦來到百分之二十五、暗紅色蛤蜊的百分之二十。

【還能怎麼說】

- Researchers are studying rare crocodiles that have been **dominating** Ghost Lake and do not have any natural enemies.

  研究人員正在研究一直以來都佔領幽靈湖泊的罕見鱷魚，且其沒有任何天敵。

- Zebra snakes **dominating** in the region have shown no signs of abating, and pretty soon there will be lacking enough chameleons to feed their hungry mouths.

  佔領這個地區的斑馬蛇沒有顯示出減少的跡象，而不久之後，這裡就會缺乏足夠數量的變色龍來餵飽牠們飢餓之口。

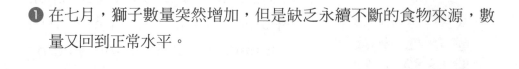
❶ 在七月,獅子數量突然增加,但是缺乏永續不斷的食物來源,數量又回到正常水平。

_____

_____

【參考答案】

There was a bulge in the number of lions in July, but without perennial food sources, the number is back to the normal.

❷ 在八月時,老虎數量暫時激增,使得科學家們興致勃勃地決定要待在這裡幾個月。

_____

_____

【參考答案】

Intrigued by the bulge in the number of tigers in August, scientists have decided to stay there for a couple of months.

❸ 僅是糖種植園的損失就預估來到 50 億元,且沒有減少的跡象。

_____

_____

【參考答案】

Losses are estimated at 5 billion dollars for the sugar plantations alone, and it shows no signs of abating.

❹ 在去年章魚的飲食中，太平洋蝦子仍舊佔據百分之五十五，接續是巨型龍蝦來到百分之二十五、暗紅色蛤蜊的百分之二十。

_____

_____

【參考答案】

Of octopuses' diet in last summer, Pacific larger shrimps still dominated at 55%, followed by giant lobsters at 25% and crimson clams at 20%.

❺ 佔領這個地區的斑馬蛇沒有顯示出減少的跡象，而不久之後，這裡就會缺乏足夠數量的變色龍來餵飽牠們飢餓之口。

_____

_____

【參考答案】

Zebra snakes dominating in the region have shown no signs of abating, and pretty soon there will be lacking enough chameleons to feed their hungry mouths.

 **Unit 10**

Questions 1-14 Complete the summary

There was a **1.** _____ in the number of lions in July, but without perennial food sources, the number is back to the normal.

As can be seen from the graph, the **2.** _____ of the health care stock had a bulge in 2019.

3. _____ by the bulge in the number of tigers in August, scientists have decided to stay there for a couple of months.

Losses are **4.** _____ at 5 billion dollars for the sugar plantations alone, and it shows no signs of **5.** _____.

Some nations suggested that the price of these fossil records be **6.** _____ because they show no signs of abating.

The fiscal **7.** _____ of the desert village is estimated at 5 million dollars, and it shows no signs of abating.

Of octopuses' **8.** _____ in last summer, Pacific larger shrimps still **9.** _____ at 55%, followed by giant lobsters at 25% and **10.** _____ clams at 20%.

Researchers are studying rare **11.** _____ that have been dominating Ghost Lake and do not have any **12.** _____ enemies.

Zebra snakes **13.** _____ in the region have shown no signs of abating, and pretty soon there will be lacking enough chameleons to feed their **14.** _____ mouths.

Boxes

A deficit

B intrigued

C abating

D estimated

E diet

F pegged down

G dominated

H crimson

I natural

J crocodiles

K dominating

L hungry

M bulge

N growth

參考答案

1. M	2. N	3. B	4. D	5. C	6. F	7. A
8. E	9. G	10. H	11. J	12. I	13. K	14. L

101

雅思百變圖表題字彙

Unit 11

★ 單元概述

　　第一個字彙介紹了高階的字彙 zoom，表示「飆升」，可以在線條圖和曲線圖中搭配先前介紹過的 slump 運用，表達會更出色。例句中還搭配了股票和價格等，可以記起來。第二個字彙也是高階的字彙且考生較少用到，它還是名詞所以更不好使用，但是在表達某些物品的增值等就能用上，可以參考這幾個例句的用法，像是例句中的黃金價值的增值幅度。最後介紹的是百分比 percentage，如果適時使用其實效果還不錯。在句型變化上可以記下搭配了 less than a third…的第三個例句，也是高分句型的表達，而非僅是使用簡單句。

圖表題高分字彙 ▶ *MP3 011*

【31. zoom（價格或銷售額）猛漲；飆升】

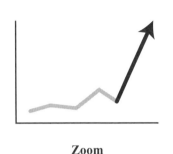

Zoom

- Last year, Best Cinema's deficits **zoomed** from 5 million dollars to 500 million dollars, noticeable growth of 100%.

  去年，倍斯特影視的赤字從 500 萬元飆升至 5 億元，顯著成長了百分之一百。

【還能怎麼說】

- The price of brown wetland dragons **zoomed** from 1 million dollars to 1 billion dollars because they can be used to guard war zones.

  棕色沼澤恐龍的價格從 1 百萬元飆升至 10 億元，因為牠們能被用於守護戰區。

- Tech stocks had a rebound, making the shares **zoom**, whereas energy stocks slumped to a new low.

  科技股有了反彈，讓股票飆升，而能源股卻降至新低點。

103

Appreciation

【**32. appreciation** （價格，價值等的）上漲，增值】

■ There has been little **appreciation** in the value of gold recently.
近期，黃金價值的增值幅度是微乎其微的。

【還能怎麼說】

■ Due to the archaeologist's excavation on July 18, the dragon tribe is now acknowledging these fossilized flowers, prompting the **appreciation** in the value of other plants.
由於考古學家在 7 月 18 日的挖掘，恐龍部落現在承認這些化石花朵，助長了其他植物價值的增值。

■ The archaeologist has denied there is **appreciation** in the value of these sculptures, but poachers living at the Dragon Gate are not fully convinced.
考古學家已經否認這些雕刻的價值有所增值，但是居住在恐龍入口的盜獵者不全然相信。

Percentage

【**33. percentage** 百分比】

■ The **percentage** of tiger cubs depending entirely on their mothers after two years has risen to 15% from 3% in 2015.

老虎幼獸的百分比全然仰賴牠們的母親，在兩年後數值由 2015 年的百分之三升至百分之十五。

【還能怎麼說】

■ If the **percentage** of the malaria infection does not improve, there is going to be another wave of spread among these gold-seekers.

如果瘧疾感染的百分比沒有改善，在那些淘金客中會出現另一波感染。

■ Less than a third of the dragon tribe inhabitants have been fully resistant to red dragon spider bites, so the **percentage** is quite low.

少於三分之一的恐龍部落居民已經完全具備抵禦紅色恐龍蜘蛛的噬咬，所以百分比是相當低的。

❶ 棕色沼澤恐龍的價格從 1 百萬元飆升至 10 億元，因為牠們能被用於守護戰區。

_____

_____

【參考答案】

The price of brown wetland dragons zoomed from 1 million dollars to 1 billion dollars because they can be used to guard war zones.

❷ 近期，黃金價值的增值幅度是微乎其微的。

_____

_____

【參考答案】

There has been little appreciation in the value of gold recently.

❸ 由於考古學家在 7 月 18 日的挖掘，恐龍部落現在承認這些化石花朵，助長了其他植物價值的增值。

_____

_____

【參考答案】

Due to the archaeologist's excavation on July 18, the dragon tribe is now acknowledging these fossilized flowers, prompting the appreciation in the value of other plants.

❹ 考古學家已經否認這些雕刻的價值有所增值，但是居住在恐龍入口的盜獵者不全然相信。

_____

_____

【參考答案】

The archaeologist has denied there is appreciation in the value of these sculptures, but poachers living at the Dragon Gate are not fully convinced.

❺ 老虎幼獸的百分比全然仰賴牠們的母親，在兩年後數值由 2015 年的百分之三升至百分之十五。

_____

_____

【參考答案】

The percentage of tiger cubs depending entirely on their mothers after two years has risen to 15% from 3% in 2015.

 **Unit 11**

Questions 1-14 Complete the summary

Last year, Best Cinema's deficits **1.** _____ from 5 million dollars to 500 million dollars, noticeable growth of 100%.

The price of brown **2.** _____ dragons zoomed from 1 million dollars to 1 billion dollars because they can be used to **3.** _____ war zones.

Tech stocks had a **4.** _____, making the shares zoom, whereas energy stocks **5.** _____ to a new low.

There has been little **6.** _____ in the value of gold recently.

Due to the archaeologist's **7.** _____ on July 18, the dragon tribe is now **8.** _____ these fossilized flowers, prompting the appreciation in the value of other plants.

The archaeologist has denied there is appreciation in the value of these sculptures, but **9.** _____ living at the Dragon Gate are not fully **10.** _____.

The percentage of tiger cubs depending **11.** _____ on their mothers after two years has **12.** _____ to 15% from 3% in 2015.

If the percentage of the malaria **13.** _____ does not improve, there is going to be another wave of spread among these gold-seekers.

Less than a third of the dragon tribe inhabitants have been fully
1. _____ to red dragon spider bites, so the percentage
is quite low.

Boxes

A appreciation	**B** slumped
C poachers	**D** excavation
E convinced	**F** acknowledging
G entirely	**H** zoomed
I resistant	**J** infection
K guard	**L** risen
M wetland	**N** rebound

參考答案

1. H	2. M	3. K	4. N	5. B	6. A	7. D
8. F	9. C	10. E	11. G	12. L	13. J	14. I

雅思百變
圖表題字彙

Unit 12

★ 單元概述

　　第一個字彙介紹了常見的字彙 between，不過還是很看考生本身的運用能力，它能夠靈活的搭配出先前所介紹的 hover or vacillate，表示在某個數值間擺動，例句中則搭配了 grow 和 spike，以及單純指兩個年份之間，建議這三個例句的用法都要會。第二個字彙介紹了表達「相當於」的 represent，可以參考例句的使用。最後介紹的是 price，一定要會使用 be priced at 的用法，例句中則包含了現在式和未來式的用法。

圖表題高分字彙 ▶ *MP3 012*

【**34. between** 在...之間】

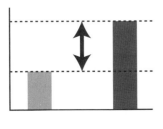

Between

■ Most estimates predict that golden roses to grow **between** 50% to 56% over the next 3 years.
大多數的預估預測在接下來的 3 年，金色玫瑰的成長介於 50%至 56%的幅度。

【還能怎麼說】

■ Last winter, temperatures spiked to **between** 42 and 45 degrees for the following days, thawing abundant snow that covers fossilized spiders.
去年冬天，溫度於接下來的幾天增至 42 度到 45 度之間，融化了覆蓋在石化蜘蛛上豐厚的雪。

■ **Between** 2000 and 2002, there was a sharp decline in the number of giant lobsters, and divers were disappointed at the scene when they filmed the video.
在 2000 和 2002 之間，巨型龍蝦的數量有急遽的下降，而當潛水客們拍攝視頻時對於此景感到大失所望。

Represent

【**35. represent** 意味著；等於；相當於】

■ The figure in the 2018 bar graph **represented** a 50% decrease on the 2019 pie chart.
該數值在 2018 年的條狀圖中代表著 2019 年圓餅圖中有著 50%的減少。

【還能怎麼說】

■ People visiting the archaeological site **represent** more revenue for the museum.
拜訪考古遺跡的人們意味著博物館能有更多的收益。

■ Effort of getting golden dragon's eggs hatched **represents** endeavor of plucking the peculiar roses under the sea.
努力讓金色恐龍蛋孵化相當於竭力摘取海底下的稀有玫瑰。

Price

【36. price 給...定價，給...標價】

■ The macabre castle is **priced** at 1 billion dollars, and the market value shows no signs of abating.

恐怖的城堡定價是 10 億元，而在市場價值中沒有減少的跡象。

【還能怎麼說】

■ The Ghost Lake is **priced** at 2 billion dollars, but during the bidding war, the price has more than tripled.

幽靈湖泊定價在 20 億元，但是在競價期間，價格增加了超過三倍。

■ The ghost ship miniature will be **priced** at 60,000 dollars, and the number above that will be used as the donation.

幽靈船的迷你模型將定價在 6 萬元，而超過此金額將會用於捐贈用途。

❶ 大多數的預估預測在接下來的 3 年，金色玫瑰的成長介於 50%至 56%的幅度。

_____

_____

【參考答案】

Most estimates predict that golden roses to grow between 50% to 56% over the next 3 years.

❷ 去年冬天，溫度於接下來的幾天增至 42 度到 45 度之間，融化了覆蓋在石化蜘蛛上豐厚的雪。

_____

_____

【參考答案】

Last winter, temperatures spiked to between 42 and 45 degrees for the following days, thawing abundant snow that covers fossilized spiders.

❸ 拜訪考古遺跡的人們意味著博物館能有更多的收益。

_____

_____

【參考答案】

People visiting the archaeological site represent more revenue for the museum.

❹ 努力讓金色恐龍蛋孵化相當於竭力摘取海底下的稀有玫瑰。

_____

_____

【參考答案】

Effort of getting golden dragon's eggs hatched represents endeavor of plucking the peculiar roses under the sea.

❺ 幽靈湖泊定價在 20 億元，但是在競價期間，價格增加了超過三倍。

_____

_____

【參考答案】

The Ghost Lake is priced at 2 billion dollars, but during the bidding war, the price has more than tripled.

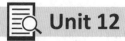 **Unit 12**

Questions 1-14 Complete the summary

Most estimates predict that golden roses to **1.** _____
between 50% to 56% over the next 3 years.

Last winter, temperatures **2.** _____ to between 42 and
45 degrees for the following days, thawing **3.** _____
snow that covers fossilized spiders.

Between 2000 and 2002, there was a **4.** _____ decline
in the number of giant lobsters, and divers were **5.** _____
__ at the scene when they filmed the video.

The figure in the 2018 bar graph represented a 50% **6.** _____
_____ on the 2019 pie chart.

People visiting the **7.** _____ site represent more
revenue for the museum.

Effort of getting golden dragon's eggs hatched represents **8.** __
_____ of plucking the **9.** _____ roses under the
sea.

The macabre **10.** _____ is priced at 1 billion dollars,
and the market **11.** _____ shows no signs of abating.

The **12.** _____ Lake is priced at 2 billion dollars, but
during the **13.** _____ war, the price has more than
tripled.

The ghost ship **14.** _____ will be priced at 60,000 dollars, and the number above that will be used as the donation.

Boxes

A Ghost   **B** grow

C spiked   **D** endeavor

E archaeological   **F** abundant

G disappointed   **H** peculiar

I castle   **J** sharp

K value   **L** decrease

M miniature   **N** bidding

參考答案

1. B	2. C	3. F	4. J	5. G	6. L	7. E
8. D	9. H	10. I	11. K	12. A	13. N	14. M

雅思百變 圖表題字彙

Unit 13

★ 單元概述

　　第一個字彙介紹了高分字彙 meteoric，表示顯著的成長，這跟另一本書介紹過的 balloon 等都是很實用的字彙。比用 remarkable increase 更佳。在第三個例句中也有更靈活的搭配，例如分別用到 surge 和 increase，考生也可以在自己學過的字彙中搭配並造句。第一個字彙也是鮮少使用上的高分字彙 slacken，能跟之前介紹過的 slump 等或是 meteoric 搭配使用，在有數值起伏波動的圖表中，特別有用。最後介紹的也是高分字彙 wane，考生太常使用 reduce 或 decrease 等字，較少用到 wane 或 dwindle，建議可以多用這類的字彙。

圖表題高分字彙 ▶ *MP3 013*

【37. meteoric 發展迅速的，扶搖直上】

■ Due to a surge in the number of lobsters in the region, the number of octopuses and squids has had a **meteoric** rise.

由於該地區的龍蝦數量的激增，章魚和烏賊數量也有突飛猛進的成長。

Meteoric

【還能怎麼說】

■ The government has since recommended that a third of fruit yields be distributed to regions that had a **meteoric** rise in livestock.

自從那時候起，政府就推薦三分之一的水果產量分配給在家畜發展迅速的地區。

■ Due to a fatal surge in cases of golden snake bites, hospitals in the dragon town had a **meteoric** increase, culminating in the number of 98 in 2019.

由於金蛇咬傷案例的猛然激增，恐龍鎮上的醫院發展迅速，在 2019 年數量達到 98 間醫院的巔峰。

Slacken

【**38. slacken** 放慢，放鬆，減緩】

■ As can be seen from the graph, the growth of the tech stock **slackened** during the Christmas.
如圖表所示，科技股的成長在聖誕節期間減緩。

【還能怎麼說】

■ Many countries have **slackened** covid-19 lockdowns because of the rising number of people getting vaccinated.
許多國家已經放緩新冠肺炎的封鎖，因為接種疫苗人數持續上升。

■ The government has **slackened** the policy of capturing giant lobsters, so divers now are freely to dive down and capture them in every season.
政府已經放緩捕捉巨型龍蝦的政策，所以潛水客現在可以在每個季節自由地往下潛水以捕獲牠們。

【39. wane 衰減；減弱 】

■ The profit margins for the heavy coat are **waning**, so the company has to rely on other products to compensate for the overall operating cost.

厚重大衣的淨利率正衰減，所以公司已經仰賴其他產品以補償整體的營運支出。

Wane

【還能怎麼說】

■ Kidney failures triggered by five-colored spider bites have been **waning** because the effect of the vaccine is working.

由五彩蜘蛛咬傷引起的腎衰竭持續減弱中，因為疫苗正發揮效果。

■ Signs of golden crab stings include heart diseases, **waning** heartbeat, and breathlessness, so it is advisable to wear heavy gloves when grabbing them.

金色螃蟹螫咬的跡象，包含了心臟疾病、逐漸減弱的心跳和無呼吸徵兆，所以抓牠們時，建議要戴厚重的手套。

❶ 自從那時候起，政府就推薦三分之一的水果產量分配給在家畜發
展迅速的地區。

_____

_____

【參考答案】

The government has since recommended that a third of fruit
yields be distributed to regions that had a meteoric rise in
livestock.

❷ 由於金蛇咬傷案例的猛然激增，恐龍鎮上的醫院發展迅速，在
2019 年數量達到 98 間醫院的巔峰。

_____

_____

【參考答案】

Due to a fatal surge in cases of golden snake bites, hospitals in the
dragon town had a meteoric increase, culminating in the number
of 98 in 2019.

❸ 許多國家已經放緩新冠肺炎的封鎖，因為接種疫苗人數持續上
升。

_____

_____

【參考答案】

Many countries have slackened covid-19 lockdowns because of the rising number of people getting vaccinated.

❹ 厚重大衣的淨利率正衰減，所以公司已經仰賴其他產品以補償整體的營運支出。

_____

_____

【參考答案】

The profit margins for the heavy coat are waning, so the company has to rely on other products to compensate for the overall operating cost.

❺ 金色螃蟹螯咬的跡象，包含了心臟疾病、逐漸減弱的心跳和無呼吸徵兆，所以抓牠們時，建議要戴厚重的手套。

_____

_____

【參考答案】

Signs of golden crab stings include heart diseases, waning heartbeat, and breathlessness, so it is advisable to wear heavy gloves when grabbing them.

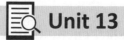

Questions 1-14 Complete the summary

Due to a **1.** _____ in the number of lobsters in the region, the number of octopuses and squids has had a **2.** _____ rise.

The government has since **3.** _____ that a third of fruit yields be **4.** _____ to regions that had a meteoric rise in livestock.

Due to a **5.** _____ surge in cases of golden snake bites, hospitals in the dragon town had a meteoric increase, **6.** _____ in the number of 98 in 2019.

As can be seen from the graph, the growth of the tech stock **7.** _____ during the Christmas.

Many countries have slackened covid-19 **8.** _____ because of the rising number of people getting **9.** _____ __.

The government has slackened the policy of **10.** _____ giant lobsters, so divers now are freely to dive down and capture them in every season.

The profit **11.** _____ for the heavy coat are waning, so the company has to rely on other products to compensate for the overall operating cost.

Kidney failures **12.** _____ by five-colored spider bites have been waning because the **13.** _____ of the vaccine is working.

Signs of golden crab stings include heart diseases, waning heartbeat, and **14.** _____, so it is advisable to wear heavy gloves when grabbing them.

Part 2

雅思精選小作文範文

Boxes

A margins	**B** recommended
C meteoric	**D** capturing
E lockdowns	**F** culminating
G distributed	**H** surge
I vaccinated	**J** fatal
K effect	**L** slackened
M breathlessness	**N** triggered

參考答案

1. H	2. C	3. B	4. G	5. J	6. F	7. L
8. E	9. I	10. D	11. A	12. N	13. K	14. M

雅思百變
圖表題字彙

Unit 14

★ 單元概述

　　第一個字彙介紹的是 astounding，可以加在數值或名詞前，讓讀者或考官感受到增加或減少的幅度，可以用於 decrease 或 increase 等字前面，多使用這類的形容詞也能使分數更高些。第二個字是常見字彙 top，但是關於其當動詞的用法，在考生範文中幾乎沒出現，通常很多字彙大家都背過但在使用的靈活度上很侷限，建議可以多用這類的字，代表很多常見字彙的動詞和名詞用法你都掌握了。這個字也能跟先前介紹過的 surpass 輪替使用。最後介紹的是高分字彙 tumble，可以跟前面介紹過許多漲幅或銳減的字彙搭配運用，讓整體表達更令人驚艷。

圖表題高分字彙 ▶ *MP3 014*

【40. astounding 令人震驚的；使人驚駭的】

Astounding

■ An **astounding** 70% of these stocks recommended by Best Analysis are profitable.

由倍斯特分析公司所推薦的這些股票有百分之七十的驚人成長，利潤頗豐。

【還能怎麼說】

■ Gold-diggers have found an **astounding** amount of gold that weighs around 20 kilos, making others exceedingly jealous.

淘金客已經發現了重達大約 20 公斤、量令人驚駭的黃金，讓其他人忌妒萬分。

■ The country has an **astounding** 90% vaccination rate, easily breaking the herd immunity threshold.

這個國家有著驚人的百分之九十的接種率，輕易地達到了群體免疫門檻。

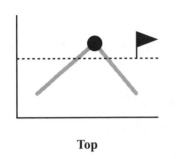

Top

【41. top 高於；超過；勝過】

- Best Cinema's profits have **topped** 2 billion dollars in the third quarter, the drastic increase since 2021.

  倍斯特影視的利潤在第三季時已經高於 20 億元，這是自從 2021 年後有急遽的增加。

【還能怎麼說】

- The price of golden large crabs **topped** 500 dollars per kilo last year, and fishermen are expecting a high turnover this year.

  金色大型螃蟹去年每公斤的價格超過 500 元，而在今年，漁夫期待會有高的營業額。

- Prices **topping** more than 1 billion will result in no buyers, so a fair bidding price is very important.

  超過 10 億元的開價會導致沒有買家，所以公平的競價是非常重要的。

Tumble

【42. tumble（價值）暴跌，驟降】

■ Due to unforeseen factors, tech stocks have **tumbled** recently, making investors moody.
由於無法預測的因素，科技股在近期暴跌，讓投資客鬱鬱寡歡。

【還能怎麼說】

■ Those designed traps are estimated to catch up to at least 100 golden snakes, but the price unbelievably **tumbled** in the morning.
那些設計的陷阱估計會抓到至少 100 條金蛇，但是在早上，價格卻令人難以置信地暴跌了。

■ Golden giant bees touching blue tulips will have a change in physical appearance, making them less likely to be purchased, and the price will inevitably **tumble**.
接觸到藍色鬱金香的金色巨型蜜蜂會在身體外表發生變化，讓牠們更為滯銷，而價格也無可避免地暴跌了。

整合能力強化 ❷ 單句中譯英演練

❶ 這個國家有著驚人的百分之九十的接種率,輕易地達到了群體免疫門檻。

_____

_____

【參考答案】

The country has an astounding 90% vaccination rate, easily breaking the herd immunity threshold.

❷ 金色大型螃蟹去年每公斤的價格超過 500 元,而在今年,漁夫期待會有高的營業額。

_____

_____

【參考答案】

The price of golden large crabs topped 500 dollars per kilo last year, and fishermen are expecting a high turnover this year.

❸ 超過 10 億元的開價會導致沒有買家,所以公平的競價是非常重要的。

_____

_____

【參考答案】

Prices topping more than 1 billion will result in no buyers, so a fair bidding price is very important.

❹ 由於無法預測的因素，科技股在近期暴跌，讓投資客鬱鬱寡歡。

_____

_____

【參考答案】

Due to unforeseen factors, tech stocks have tumbled recently, making investors moody.

❺ 接觸到藍色鬱金香的金色巨型蜜蜂會在身體外表發生變化，讓牠們更為滯銷，而價格也無可避免地暴跌了。

_____

_____

【參考答案】

Golden giant bees touching blue tulips will have a change in physical appearance, making them less likely to be purchased, and the price will inevitably tumble.

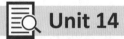 **Unit 14**

Questions 1-14 Complete the summary

An **1.** _____ 70% of these Stocks recommended by Best Analysis are profitable.

Gold-diggers have found an astounding amount of gold that **2.** _____ around 20 kilos, making others exceedingly **3.** __ _____.

The country has an astounding 90% **4.** _____ rate, easily breaking the herd immunity threshold.

Best Cinema's profits have **5.** _____ 2 billion dollars in the third quarter, the drastic increase since 2021.

The price of golden **6.** _____ crabs topped 500 dollars per kilo last year, and fishermen are expecting a high **7.** _____ _____ this year.

Prices topping more than 1 billion will result in no **8.** _____ ____, so a **9.** _____ bidding price is very important.

Due to unforeseen factors, tech stocks have **10.** _____ recently, making investors moody.

Those **11.** _____ traps are estimated to catch up to at least 100 golden snakes, but the price **12.** _____ tumbled in the morning.

Golden giant bees touching blue tulips will have a change in physical **13.** _____, making them less likely to be **14.** __ _____, and the price will inevitably tumble.

Boxes

A fair

B large

C vaccination

D jealous

E buyers

F topped

G designed

H turnover

I tumbled

J unbelievably

K appearance

L purchased

M astounding

N weighs

參考答案

1. M	2. N	3. D	4. C	5. F	6. B	7. H
8. E	9. A	10. I	11. G	12. J	13. K	14. L

雅思百變
圖表題字彙

Unit 15

★ 單元概述

　　第一個字彙介紹的是高分字彙 lag，它像是先前介紹過的 sag 等非母語人士更少用在圖表題作文的字彙，在例句中更有表達出落後其他債卷並搭配現在完成式用法的部分，建議背起來。第二個介紹的是常見字彙 rise，但要很注意在時態上的使用，例句中介紹了分別搭配現在完成式和過去完成式的用法，這個字彙雖然大家都會但真的運用得好的考生確實不多，可以把這幾個例句都背起來。第三個字彙要介紹的也是常見字彙 fall，第一個例句中具體描述了數值且搭配過去完成式的用法，要靈活使用這個字確實也不太容易。另外還要注意的是這個字的三態變化。

圖表題高分字彙 ▶ *MP3 015*

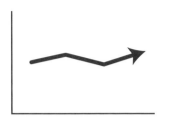

Lag

【**43. lag** 緩慢移動；掉隊，滯後】

■ Government bonds have consistently **lagged** other bonds, so investors have to be very patient.

政府債卷持續性地落後其他債卷，所以投資客必須要非常有耐心。

【還能怎麼說】

■ With industries that have grown more dependent on Best Zoo, ABC Zoo has **lagged** far behind, causing its shares to noticeably sink below the normal range.

隨著產業越來越仰賴倍斯特動物園，ABC 動物園落後更甚，造成股票有顯著下跌，低於正常水平。

■ A continued decline in Best Circus stock prices can make its growing advantages debilitating and eventually **lag** behind its rival.

倍斯特馬戲團股票持續的下跌可能讓成長的優勢逐漸減弱，而最終落後其競爭對手。

【44. rise 上升；升高；升起】

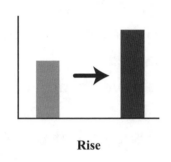

Rise

■ Best Aquarium 2239 has **risen** almost 25% since last April, and stock analysts are encouraging people to invest more.

自從去年 4 月開始，倍斯特水族館 2239（股市代碼）已經上升了百分之二十五，而股票分析師正慫恿人們投資更多。

【還能怎麼說】

■ By August 2017, the number had **risen** to 54% thanks in large parts to the education given by the health experts.

在 2017 年八月，數量升至百分之五十四，有很大部分有多虧保健專家授予的教育。

■ A handful of marine farmers have begun rejecting black lobsters as payment because the number of black lobsters has been significantly **risen** recently.

少數海洋農夫已經開始拒絕使用黑色龍蝦來付款的易物行為，因為黑色龍蝦的數量在近期有顯著的增幅。

【45. fall（規模、數量或力量）減少，降低】

■ A November survey found that health care stocks **had fallen** to the lowest of 2.5%, compared with the highest 63.5% in 2012.

在 11 月的調查報告發現，比起在 2015 年時百分之六十三點五的高點，健康照護的股份降至百分之二點五，來到了最低點。

Fall

【還能怎麼說】

■ Previous research shows that tech stocks are at increased risk of getting undersold, and they are expected to **fall** to at least 12.5%.

先前的研究顯示出科技股受到拋售的風險日益增加，預期會跌至至少百分之十二點五。

■ If any of these predictions were correct, financial stocks would be bound to **fall** in a few hours.

如果任何關於這些預測都是正確的，金融股一定會在幾小時內下跌。

整合能力強化 ② 單句中譯英演練

❶ 政府債卷持續性地落後其他債卷,所以投資客必須要非常有耐心。

_____

_____

【參考答案】

Government bonds have consistently lagged other bonds, so investors have to be very patient.

❷ 自從去年 4 月開始,倍斯特水族館 2239(股市代碼)已經上升了百分之二十五,而股票分析師正慫恿人們投資更多。

_____

_____

【參考答案】

Best Aquarium 2239 has risen almost 25% since last April, and stock analysts are encouraging people to invest more.

❸ 少數海洋農夫已經開始拒絕使用黑色龍蝦來付款的易物行為,因為黑色龍蝦的數量在近期有顯著的增幅。

_____

_____

【參考答案】

A handful of marine farmers have begun rejecting black lobsters as payment because the number of black lobsters has been significantly risen recently.

❹ 在 11 月的調查報告發現，比起在 2015 年時百分之六十三點五的高點，健康照護的股份降至百分之二點五，來到了最低點。

_____

_____

【參考答案】

A November survey found that health care stocks had fallen to the lowest of 2.5%, compared with the highest 63.5% in 2012.

❺ 如果任何關於這些預測都是正確的，金融股一定會在幾小時內下跌。

_____

_____

【參考答案】

If any of these predictions were correct, financial stocks would be bound to fall in a few hours.

Questions 1-14 Complete the summary

Government bonds have consistently **1.** _____ other bonds, so investors have to be very patient.

With industries that have grown more **2.** _____ on Best Zoo, ABC Zoo has lagged far behind, causing its shares to **3.** _____ _____ sink below the normal range.

A continued decline in Best Circus stock prices can make its growing advantages **4.** _____ and eventually lag behind its **5.** _____.

Best Aquarium 2239 **6.** _____ almost 25% since last April, and stock analysts are **7.** _____ people to invest more.

By August 2017, the number **8.** _____ to 54% thanks in large parts to the **9.** _____ given by the health experts.

A handful of marine farmers have begun rejecting black lobsters as **10.** _____ because the number of black lobsters has been significantly risen recently.

A November survey found that health care stocks **11.** _____ _____ to the lowest of 2.5%, compared with the highest 63.5% in 2012.

Previous research shows that tech stocks are at **12.** _____ ____ risk of getting **13.** _____, and they are expected to fall to at least 12.5%.

If any of these **14.** _____ were correct, financial stocks would be bound to fall in a few hours.

Boxes

A increased	**B** dependent
C noticeably	**D** rival
E debilitating	**F** lagged
G had risen	**H** has risen
I had fallen	**J** education
K undersold	**L** payment
M predictions	**N** encouraging

參考答案

1. F	2. B	3. C	4. E	5. D	6. H	7. N
8. G	9. J	10. L	11. I	12. A	13. K	14. M

雅思百變
圖表題字彙

Unit 16

★ 單元概述

　　第一個字彙介紹了高分字彙 hefty，表示「可觀的」，考生在範文中幾乎未用到這個字彙，可以搭配數值，這個字彙的第二個例句也很值得學習，搭配了 only a small proportion of⋯，建議可以多用不同文法書上常見的句型，讓範文更出色。第二個字彙介紹了 outstanding，大家最知道的是這個字彙當「傑出的」的意思，但它也有「顯著的」的意思，且比 noticeable 或 remarkable 更不常在範文中出現，考生可以多用這類的字彙，例句中還有搭配到 improvement 或 effect，使用很靈巧，建議都學起來。最後要介紹的是 mediocre，這個字彙較少出現在範文中，可以跟 hefty 或 outstanding 一起使用，表達出圖表數值的變化，或是搭配 fluctuate 等字以描述出數值沒有什麼變化或波動。

圖表題高分字彙 ▶ *MP3 016*

【46. hefty（數額、尺寸、力量等）大的，可觀的】

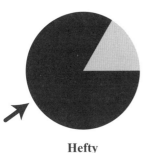

Hefty

■ By purchasing this investment portfolio, you are able to get a **hefty** 12.5% return, much better than interest rates of certified deposits.

藉由購買這款投資組合，你能夠獲得可觀的 12.5%的回報，比起特定的存款組合利率要來得高。

【還能怎麼說】

■ At present, only a small proportion of ten-colored spiders with the injection have a **hefty** effect, so extracting their venom for use is still a long way to go.

現在僅小部分有注射的十彩蜘蛛有可觀的效果，所以取出牠們的毒性以供使用仍有一段漫長的路要走。

■ Financial analysts are guaranteeing that investors will get a **hefty** 28% profit per month, according to the report.

金融分析師保證，投資客每個月會獲得百分之二十八的可觀利潤，根據報導。

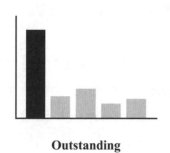

Outstanding

【**47. outstanding** 凸出的;顯著的】

- Over the past 7 years, Best Museum's stocks have averaged an **outstanding** 25.5% profit, whereas its rival has fallen far behind.

  過去 7 年間,倍斯特博物館的股份平均有顯著的 25.5%利潤,而其競爭對手卻大幅落後。

【還能怎麼說】

- With men being more likely to get bitten by venomous octopuses, researchers have begun using the antibody that will have an **outstanding** effect on the removal of the toxin.

  隨著男性更易於受到有毒章魚的咬傷,研究人員已經使用了有顯著效果的抗體以移除毒性。

- About 47% of people getting vaccines that contain spider venom have exhibited an **outstanding** improvement in lung diseases.

  大約百分之四十七接種含有蜘蛛毒液疫苗的人顯示出對肺部疾病有明顯改善。

144

【48. mediocre 普通的；平庸的】

■ Over the past 3 years, Best Amusement Park's rate of return has averaged a **mediocre** 3.5%, making investors hesitant for the further investment.

過去三年間，倍斯特遊樂園的回報率平均有平平無奇的百分之三點五，讓投資客們對於進一步的投資感到猶豫不前。

Mediocre

【還能怎麼說】

■ In the case of malaria, stock prices recuperated about a year later after the diagnosed cases started dropping, implying that stocks with **mediocre** performance can still be strong.

在瘧疾的案例中，診斷出的案例開始下滑後，股價約在一年後有反彈，暗示出有著平庸表現的股票仍可以有強勁發展。

■ A wave of cancellations by online shoppers have added insult into injury to the companies with **mediocre** sales records.

線上購物者的一波訂單取消對銷售紀錄一般的公司是雪上加霜的。

❶ 藉由購買這款投資組合，你能夠獲得可觀的 12.5%的回報，比起特定的存款組合利率要來得高。

_____

_____

【參考答案】

By purchasing this investment portfolio, you are able to get a hefty 12.5% return, much better than interest rates of certified deposits.

❷ 現在僅小部分有注射的十彩蜘蛛有可觀的效果，所以取出牠們的毒性以供使用仍有一段漫長的路要走。

_____

_____

【參考答案】

At present, only a small proportion of ten-colored spiders with the injection have a hefty effect, so extracting their venom for use is still a long way to go.

❸ 大約百分之四十七接種含有蜘蛛毒液疫苗的人顯示出對肺部疾病有明顯改善。

_____

_____

【參考答案】
About 47% of people getting vaccines that contain spider venom have exhibited an outstanding improvement in lung diseases.

❹ 過去三年間，倍斯特遊樂園的回報率平均有平平無奇的百分之三點五，讓投資客們對於進一步的投資感到猶豫不前。

_____

_____

【參考答案】
Over the past 3 years, Best Amusement Park's rate of return has averaged a mediocre 3.5%, making investors hesitant for the further investment.

❺ 在瘧疾的案例中，診斷出的案例開始下滑後，股價約在一年後有反彈，暗示出有著平庸表現的股票仍可以有強勁發展。

_____

_____

【參考答案】
In the case of malaria, stock prices recuperated about a year later after the diagnosed cases started dropping, implying that stocks with mediocre performance can still be strong.

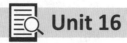

Questions 1-14 Complete the summary

By purchasing this **1.** _____ portfolio, you are able to get a hefty 12.5% return, much better than interest rates of certified **2.** _____.

At present, only a small proportion of ten-colored spiders with the injection have a **3.** _____ effect, so extracting their **4.** _____ for use is still a long way to go.

Financial analysts are **5.** _____ that investors will get a hefty 28% **6.** _____ per month, according to the report.

Over the past 7 years, Best Museum's stocks have averaged an **7.** _____ 25.5% profit, whereas its rival has fallen far behind.

With men being more likely to get bitten by **8.** _____ octopuses, researchers have begun using the antibody that will have an outstanding effect on the **9.** _____ of the toxin.

About 47% of people getting vaccines that **10.** _____ spider venom have exhibited an outstanding improvement in lung diseases.

Over the past 3 years, Best Amusement Park's rate of return has averaged a **11.** _____ 3.5%, making investors **12.** _____ for the further investment.

In the case of malaria, stock prices **13.** _____ about a year later after the diagnosed cases started dropping, implying that stocks with mediocre performance can still be strong.

A wave of **14.** _____ by online shoppers have added insult into injury to the companies with mediocre sales records.

Boxes

A contain
B venomous
C cancellations
D removal
E hefty
F recuperated
G mediocre
H hesitant
I guaranteeing
J profit
K venom
L investment
M deposits
N outstanding

參考答案

1. L	2. M	3. E	4. K	5. I	6. J	7. N
8. B	9. D	10. A	11. G	12. H	13. F	14. C

雅思百變
圖表題字彙

Unit 17

⭐ 單元概述

　　第一個字介紹的是高分字彙 sluggish，可以跟先前介紹的 lag 輪替使用，這個字的幾個例句也很值得學習，尤其是第二個例句中用上了 half of whom…，或是第三個例句中僅僅用來修飾名詞。第二個字彙要介紹的是 improve，是個常見的字，但在搭配數值上，鮮少有考生使用，例句中包含了分別搭配數值和現在完成式以及過去完成式用法，建議都記起來，避免使用錯誤。最後要介紹的是高分字彙 slash，當中包含了搭配百分比的使用，可以用於數值和工作部分，例如失業率等圖表，能比較出差異，表達出兩圖表間數值的顯著變化。

圖表題高分字彙 ▶ MP3 017

【49. sluggish 行動緩慢的；遲緩的】

■ Over the past five years, the peculiar insect market has been **sluggish** because of extreme weather conditions.

過去 5 年間，因為極端的天候條件，稀有昆蟲的市場已遲緩。

Sluggish

【還能怎麼說】

■ Researchers have been using ten-colored spiders aged between 12 months old to 18 months old, half of whom have not shown the **sluggish** performance, to treat arthritis.

研究人員一直以來是使用年紀約 12 個月大至 18 個月大的十彩蜘蛛，當中有半數沒有顯示出遲緩的表現，以治療風濕症。

■ There is no proven treatment for ten-colored snake bites, and the symptom includes a **sluggish** walk, followed by an acute heart failure.

十彩蛇的咬傷沒有證實有效的療方，而症狀包含了緩慢地行走，跟接續的急促心臟衰竭。

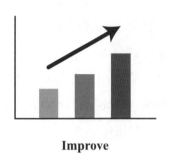

Improve

【 **50. improve** 改進，改善 】

■ The hourly wage of strawberry farmers rose 25% over the decade from 2016, but quality **improved** by 3.5%.

草莓農夫每小時的薪資在過去 2016 年間有著 25%的增長，但是其品質卻僅只有 3.5%的改進。

....

【 還能怎麼說 】

■ Only 5% of people owned foreign currencies, and the situation has **improved** with the release of more educational investment programs.

僅有百分之五的人持有外幣，但情況因為更多投資教育計畫的推出而有所改善。

■ By November 2016, the rate had risen to 15% because more people were more aware of the **improved** scarce spiders hidden under the snow.

到了 2016 年 11 月，比率升至百分之十五，因為更多人都意識到藏在雪底下的改良版的罕見蜘蛛。

....

【51. slash 大幅削減，大幅減少（金錢、工作等）】

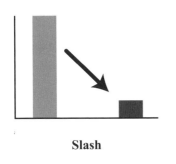

Slash

■ The price of the rare pinky spiders has been remarkably **slashed** by 70% because of increasingly rampant clones.

稀奇的粉色蜘蛛的價格已顯著地大幅削減的 70%，因為日益增加的猖獗的複製品的出現。

【還能怎麼說】

■ The tornado is believed to have caused 1 billion economic losses and **slashed** production by 250,000 tons, equivalent to 25% of Europe's exports.

颶風被視為導致 10 億元經濟損失的原因，且產量大幅削弱了 25 萬噸，等同於歐洲出口量的 25%。

■ The profit for these golden crabs has been significantly **slashed**, a sharp contrast to a year earlier.

這些金色螃蟹的利潤有顯著的大幅削減，跟前一年相比很明顯。

❶ 研究人員一直以來是使用年紀約 12 個月大至 18 個月大的十彩蜘蛛，當中有半數沒有顯示出遲緩的表現，以治療風濕症。

_____

_____

【參考答案】

Researchers have been using ten-colored spiders aged between 12 months old to 18 months old, half of whom have not shown the sluggish performance, to treat arthritis.

❷ 草莓農夫每小時的薪資在過去 2016 年間有著 25%的增長，但是其品質卻僅只有 3.5%的改進。

_____

_____

【參考答案】

The hourly wage of strawberry farmers rose 25% over the decade from 2016, but quality improved by 3.5%.

❸ 僅有百分之五的人持有外幣，但情況因為更多投資教育的計畫推出而有所改善。

_____

_____

【參考答案】

Only 5% of people owned foreign currencies, and the situation has improved with the release of more educational investment programs.

❹ 稀奇的粉色蜘蛛的價格已顯著地大幅削減的 70%，因為日益增加的猖獗的複製品的出現。

_____

_____

【參考答案】

The price of the rare pinky spiders has been remarkably slashed by 70% because of increasingly rampant clones.

❺ 颶風被視為導致 10 億元經濟損失的原因，且產量大幅削弱了 25 萬噸，等同於歐洲出口量的百分之二十五。

_____

_____

【參考答案】

The tornado is believed to have caused 1 billion economic losses and slashed production by 250,000 tons, equivalent to 25% of Europe's exports.

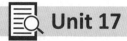

Questions 1-14 Complete the summary

Over the past five years, the peculiar insect market has been **1.** _____ because of extreme weather conditions.

Researchers have been using ten-colored spiders aged between 12 months old to 18 months old, half of **2.** _____ have not shown the sluggish performance, to **3.** _____ arthritis.

There is no **4.** _____ treatment for ten-colored snake bites, and the symptom includes a sluggish walk, followed by an **5.** _____ heart failure.

The hourly **6.** _____ of strawberry farmers rose 25% over the decade from 2016, but quality improved by 3.5%.

Only 5% of people owned foreign **7.** _____, and the situation has improved with the release of more **8.** _____ investment programs.

By November 2016, the rate had risen to 15% because more people were more aware of the **9.** _____ spiders hidden under the snow.

The price of the rare pinky spiders has been **10.** _____ slashed by 70% because of increasingly rampant **11.** _____.

The **12.** _____ is believed to have caused 1 billion economic losses and slashed **13.** _____ by 250,000 tons, equivalent to 25% of Europe's exports.

The profit for these golden crabs has been significantly slashed, a sharp **14.** _____ to a year earlier.

Boxes

A wage	**B** treat
C educational	**D** proven
E scarce	**F** currencies
G clones	**H** remarkably
I tornado	**J** production
K contrast	**L** acute
M whom	**N** sluggish

參考答案

1. N	2. M	3. B	4. D	5. L	6. A	7. F
8. C	9. E	10. H	11. G	12. I	13. J	14. K

雅思百變
圖表題字彙

Unit 18

★ 單元概述

　　第一個字彙介紹了 quadruple，可以取代像是 increase 或形容詞+increase 這樣的描述，因為更具體的表明出增長了四倍。三個例句中都有不同的用法，建議可以背第二句，在句型變化的部分能拉高不少分數。第二個字彙介紹了 climb，可以跟前面所介紹的 jump 等字搭配使用，也要注意時態的部分。最後介紹的是 dwindle，可以用於取代像是 decrease 或 reduce 等用法，因為其是較為高階的字彙，例句中則介紹了搭配百分比的部分，可以學起來，尤其是在花朵的多樣性的例句中的表達，直接使用 dwindled by X %，而非一直使用 have a slight increase/decrease。

超版有縮行距

圖表題高分字彙 ▶ *MP3 018*

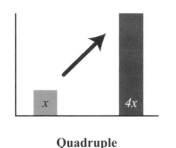

Quadruple

【**52. quadruple** （使）成為四倍；
（使）以四相乘】

■ Investment in eccentric insects **quadrupled** to 10 billion thanks largely to wealthy tycoons.
投資古怪的昆蟲成長了四倍來到 100 億元，大概要多虧富有的大亨。

【還能怎麼說】

■ Another issue is that most snake bites have occurred in children under 10, a group with a higher occurrence of getting bitten, and the total has **quadrupled** in this month.
另一個議題是，大多數的蛇咬傷都發生於十歲以下的小孩，在該族群中有更高的被咬傷機率，而這個月的總數已經增加了四倍。

■ During the meeting, fruit farmers are expecting that profits will **quadruple** to 1 billion dollars to compensate last year's catastrophic losses.
在會議期間，水果果農預期利潤會增加四倍至 10 億元以補償去年的災難性損失。

【53. climb （價格、數量等）上漲，增長，攀升】

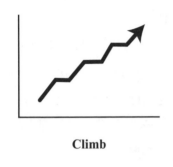

Climb

■ During the shareholder meeting, investors are expecting that profits will **climb** another 50% to 60% by 2025 to meet the company's target.

在股東會議期間，投資客正期待利潤會在 2025 年會再攀升百分之五十到六十左右以達到公司目標。

【還能怎麼說】

■ Gold prices **climbed** to a four-month high, an unusual scene in the eyes of financial experts.

黃金價格攀升至四個月的高點，在金融專家眼中是不尋常的景象。

■ Consumers who have bought government bonds are not regretting because another high-yield bond is soon to be released, so there is going to be another **climb**。

已經購買政府債卷的消費者不會感到後悔，因為另一個高收益債卷即將要推出，所以將會有另一波漲幅。

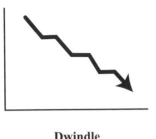

Dwindle

【 54. dwindle 減小;降低;減少 】

■ The population of the golden bears **dwindled** to a third of their original number in the fiction.
金色熊的族群數量降至小說中原本數量的三分之一。

【 還能怎麼說 】

■ In a 2008 biological analysis, researchers found that marine animals **dwindled** by 68% near the shore of Best Island, astounding many tourists.
在 2008 年的生物分析中,研究人員發現在倍斯特島嶼的海洋動物減少了百分之六十八,震驚了許多觀光客。

■ Flower diversity **dwindled** by 72% due to the introduction of peculiar plant-eating bees.
花朵的多樣性減少了百分之七十二,由於獨特的食植物蜜蜂的引進。

❶ 另一個議題是，大多數的蛇咬傷都發生於十歲以下的小孩，在該族群中有更高的被咬傷機率，而這個月的總數已經增加了四倍。

_____

_____

【參考答案】

Another issue is that most snake bites have occurred in children under 10, a group with a higher occurrence of getting bitten, and the total has quadrupled in this month.

❷ 黃金價格攀升至四個月的高點，在金融專家眼中是不尋常的景象。

_____

_____

【參考答案】

Gold prices climbed to a four-month high, an unusual scene in the eyes of financial experts.

❸ 已經購買政府債卷的消費者不會感到後悔，因為另一個高收益債卷即將要推出。

_____

_____

Part 1
雅思百變圖表題字彙

【參考答案】

Consumers who have bought government bonds are not regretting because another high-yield bond is soon to be released.

❹ 金色熊的族群數量降至小說中原本數量的三分之一。

_____

_____

【參考答案】

The population of the golden bears dwindled to a third of their original number in the fiction.

❺ 花朵的多樣性減少了百分之七十二，由於獨特的食植物蜜蜂的引進。

_____

_____

【參考答案】

Flower diversity dwindled by 72% due to the introduction of peculiar plant-eating bees.

Part 2
雅思精選小作文範文

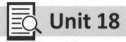

Questions 1-14 Complete the summary

Investment in **1.** _____ insects quadrupled to 10 billion thanks largely to wealthy **2.** _____.

Another issue is that most snake bites have occurred in children under 10, a group with a higher **3.** _____ of getting bitten, and the total has quadrupled in this month.

During the meeting, fruit farmers are expecting that profits will **4.** _____ to 1 billion dollars to compensate last year's **5.** _____ losses.

During the **6.** _____ meeting, investors are expecting that profits will **7.** _____ another 50% to 60% by 2025 to meet the company's target.

Gold prices climbed to a four-month high, an **8.** _____ scene in the eyes of financial experts.

Consumers who have bought **9.** _____ bonds are not regretting because another high-yield bond is soon to be **10.** ___ _____, so there is going to be another climb。

The population of the golden bears **11.** _____ to a third of their original number in the fiction.

In a 2008 biological analysis, researchers found that **12.** _____ animals dwindled by 68% near the shore of Best Island, **13.** _____ many tourists.

Flower diversity dwindled by 72% due to the **14.** _____ of peculiar plant-eating bees.

Boxes

A quadruple	**B** occurrence
C climb	**D** tycoons
E government	**F** unusual
G dwindled	**H** shareholder
I marine	**J** released
K astounding	**L** introduction
M eccentric	**N** catastrophic

參考答案

1. M	2. D	3. B	4. A	5. N	6. H	7. C
8. F	9. E	10. J	11. G	12. I	13. K	14. L

雅思百變
圖表題字彙

Unit 19

★ 單元概述

　　第一個字彙介紹了 steep，是個較為高階的字彙，能用於取代像是 have a sharp increase 等的表達，改成 have a steep increase。例句中建議背第三個例句，當中有 steep+skyrocket 等的高分表達句型。另外要介紹的是 slide，也是一個高分字彙，且考生幾乎在範文中未曾使用上，例句中有搭配股價、現在完成進行式和完成式的用法，建議三個例句的句型都要會使用。最後要介紹的也是高分字彙 snowball，可用於情勢等的擴大，再搭配其他圖表中的數值使用。建議背誦第一個和第三個例句。

圖表題高分字彙 ▶ *MP3 019*

【55. steep（上升或下降）急劇的，大起大落的】

Steep

■ There has been a **steep** decline in people visiting Best Zoo, and by 2025 visitors are expected to shrink by 50%.

參訪倍斯特動物園的人有急遽的下降，而到了 2025 年，參觀者預期會萎縮百分之五十。

【還能怎麼說】

■ There has been a **steep** increase in flower diversity in 2015, but insect diversity took a nosedive in 2016.

在 2015 年，花朵的多樣性有急遽的增幅，但是昆蟲的多樣性在 2016 年卻暴跌。

■ The price of pinky chameleons skyrocketed, reaching US 6000 per kilo, a **steep** 50% increase from 2017.

粉色變色龍的價格突然升高，達到每公斤六千美元，從 2017 年以來有百分之五十的增加。

167

Slide

【56. slide 下滑；衰落；逐漸陷入】

- Best Cinema's share **slid** from a peak above US 50.5 in September 2015 to a low of US 15.9 in October 2015.

  倍斯特影視的股價從 2015 年九月的高峰，高於 50.5 美元來下滑至到 2015 年 10 月 15.9 美元的新低。

【還能怎麼說】

- Areas with five-colored spiders have up to 70% of fierce hornets living neighboring, but the number of formidable hornets has noticeably **slidden** due to the change of hormones in the spider body.

  在有五彩蜘蛛的地區，有高達百分之七十的兇猛大黃蜂居住在附近，但是令人懼怕的大黃蜂的數量已有顯著的下滑，由於蜘蛛體內化學物質的改變。

- Sites where golden octopuses are present have fewer venomous clams and man-eating snails; nevertheless, the number of poisonous mollusks is not **sliding**.

  有金色章魚現蹤的地點有較少的有毒蛤蠣和食人蝸牛，儘管如此，有毒軟體動物的數量並沒有下滑。

【57. snowball 滾雪球般迅速增大；（程度、規模）不斷擴大】

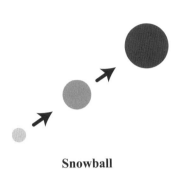

Snowball

- The situation can **snowball** into drastic wildfire, causing at least 50% of the animals living in the rainforests homeless.
情況可能像滾雪球般迅速增大至急遽的野生大火，導致至少百分之五十生活在雨林的動物都無家可歸。

【還能怎麼說】

- The situation can **snowball** into the bankruptcy of banks because consumers will be lacking faith in the banks.
情勢可能會滾雪球般迅速增大至銀行倒閉，因為消費者會對銀行缺乏信心。

- The spilling of a bottle of purple poisonous dragon blood has **snowballed** into the death of more than 2,000, almost a third of the populations of the dragon tribe.
一瓶裝有紫色有毒恐龍血的灑出已經像滾雪球般迅速增大造成超過兩千人的死亡，幾乎是恐龍部落族群的三分之一人口。

169

❶ 粉色變色龍的價格突然升高，達到每公斤六千美元，從 2017 年以
來有百分之五十的增加。

_____

_____

【參考答案】

The price of pinky chameleons skyrocketed, reaching US 6000
per kilo, a steep 50% increase from 2017.

❷ 在有五彩蜘蛛的地區，有高達百分之七十的兇猛大黃蜂居住在附
近，但是令人懼怕的大黃蜂的數量已有顯著的下滑，由於蜘蛛體
內化學物質的改變。

_____

_____

【參考答案】

Areas with five-colored spiders have up to 70% of fierce hornets
living neighboring, but the number of formidable hornets has
noticeably slidden due to the change of hormones in the spider
body.

❸ 有金色章魚現蹤的地點有較少的有毒蛤蠣和食人蝸牛，儘管如
此，有毒軟體動物的數量並沒有下滑。

_____

_____

【參考答案】
Sites where golden octopuses are present have fewer venomous clams and man-eating snails; nevertheless, the number of poisonous mollusks is not sliding.

❹ 情況可能像滾雪球般迅速增大至急遽的野生大火，導致至少百分之五十生活在雨林的動物都無家可歸。

_____

_____

【參考答案】
The situation can snowball into drastic wildfire, causing at least 50% of the animals living in the rainforests homeless.

❺ 一瓶裝有紫色有毒恐龍血的灑出已經像滾雪球般迅速增大造成超過兩千人的死亡，幾乎是恐龍部落族群的三分之一人口。

_____

_____

【參考答案】
The spilling of a bottle of purple poisonous dragon blood has snowballed into the death of more than 2,000, almost a third of the populations of the dragon tribe.

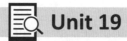

Questions 1-14 Complete the summary

There has been a **1.** _____ decline in people visiting Best Zoo, and by 2025 visitors are expected to **2.** _____ by 50%.

There has been a steep **3.** _____ in flower diversity in 2015, but insect diversity took a **4.** _____ in 2016.

The price of pinky chameleons **5.** _____, reaching US 6000 per kilo, a steep 50% increase from 2017.

Best Cinema's share **6.** _____ from a peak above US 50.5 in September 2015 to a low of US 15.9 in October 2015.

Areas with five-colored spiders have up to 70% of fierce hornets living **7.** _____, but the number of **8.** _____ hornets has noticeably slidden due to the change of hormones in the spider body.

Sites where golden octopuses are present have fewer venomous clams and man-eating **9.** _____; nevertheless, the number of **10.** _____ mollusks is not sliding.

The situation can snowball into **11.** _____ wildfire, causing at least 50% of the animals living in the rainforests homeless.

The situation can snowball into the **12.** _____ of banks because consumers will be lacking **13.** _____ in the banks.

The spilling of a bottle of purple poisonous dragon blood has snowballed into the death of more than 2,000, almost a third of the **14.** _____ of the dragon tribe.

Boxes

A faith	**B** bankruptcy
C nosedive	**D** populations
E snails	**F** skyrocketed
G drastic	**H** neighboring
I steep	**J** increase
K poisonous	**L** formidable
M shrink	**N** slid

參考答案

1. I	2. M	3. J	4. C	5. F	6. N	7. H
8. L	9. E	10. K	11. G	12. B	13. A	14. D

雅思百變
圖表題字彙

Unit 20

★ 單元概述

　　第一個要介紹的是常見的字彙 deteriorate，這個不陌生的字彙要能靈活使用確實不易，或許在大作文中有描述到某個現象的惡化，但要像例句一表明出「股價的價值下降至負百分之三十五」是較少考生能達到的字彙使用，建議背誦第一和第三個例句。第二個要介紹的是常見的 respectively，表示圖表中某兩個部分分別有哪些變化，如果對前兩個例句的用法都很熟悉的話，建議背誦第三個例句。最後要介紹的是 skyrocket，其是個高分字彙，可以跟 surge, increase, soar 等連續搭配使用，獲取寫作高分的雅思考生，都能在範文中輕易接續用上這些字彙。

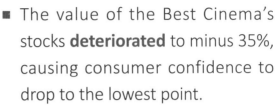

圖表題高分字彙 ▶ *MP3 020*

【**58. deteriorate** 惡化；品質（或價值）下降】

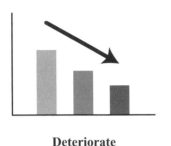

Deteriorate

■ The value of the Best Cinema's stocks **deteriorated** to minus 35%, causing consumer confidence to drop to the lowest point.

倍斯特影視的股價的價值下降至負百分之三十五，導致消費者信心降到了新低點。

【還能怎麼說】

■ While the meeting offers hope to local residents, air pollution problems have been continuing to **deteriorate** since July.

雖然會議提供了當地居民希望，空氣汙染的問題自從七月開始就一直持續惡化。

■ The survey also concluded that water salinity would drastically **deteriorate** if habitat loss problems lingered.

調查所得到的結論是水中的鹽度會急遽惡化，如果棲地損失的問題持續存在著。

175

Respectively

【59. respectively 分別地，各自地】

■ Two major circus giants, Best Circus and ABC Circus, **respectively** saw an almost 9% decline and a nearly 38% surge in revenue over the same period.

在同一時間點，兩個主要的馬戲團巨頭，倍斯特馬戲團和 ABC 馬戲團，分別目睹了收益有著幾乎百分之九的下滑和近乎百分之三十八的激增。

【還能怎麼說】

■ At this point, the authorities had found unusual snake bites **respectively** in the mountain and the lake, implying a surge in snake numbers.

在這個時候，有關當局已經分別在山上和湖泊發現了不尋常的蛇咬傷，暗示出蛇數量的激增。

■ When scientists were looking for reasons for the rise in snake numbers **respectively** in the river bank and mountain cliffs, they accidentally found an alien species.

科學家們正找尋蛇在河岸處和山崖上數量上升的原因，他們意外地發現了外來種。

Skyrocket

【60. skyrocket 猛漲;突然高升】

■ The price of golden four-eyed snakes **skyrocketed**, reaching US 60000 per kilo, a remarkable increase from 2016.
金色四眼蛇的價格猛然飆升,來到了每公斤 6 萬美元,這是從 2016 年開始有的顯著增長。

【還能怎麼說】

■ The number of purple octopuses **skyrocketed** from a low of 500 dollars to the high of 6500 dollars.
紫色章魚的數量突然從 500 元的低點升高到六千五百元的高點。

■ The rate of unvaccinated people **skyrocketed** in July, making government officials increasingly worried.
未接種人數的比例突然在七月升高,讓政府官員與日俱增地感到擔憂。

❶ 調查也結論出水中的鹽度會急遽惡化，如果棲地損失的問題持續存在著。

_____

_____

【參考答案】

The survey also concluded that water salinity would drastically deteriorate if habitat loss problems lingered.

❷ 在這個時候，有關當局已經分別在山上和湖泊發現了不尋常的蛇咬傷，暗示出蛇數量的激增。

_____

_____

【參考答案】

At this point, the authorities had found unusual snake bites respectively in the mountain and the lake, implying a surge in snake numbers.

❸ 金色四眼蛇的價格猛然飆升，來到了每公斤 6 萬美元，這是從 2016 年開始有的顯著增長。

_____

_____

【參考答案】

The price of golden four-eyed snakes skyrocketed, reaching US 60000 per kilo, a remarkable increase from 2016.

❹ 紫色章魚的數量突然從 500 元的低點升高到六千五百元的高點。

_____

_____

【參考答案】

The number of purple octopuses skyrocketed from a low of 500 dollars to the high of 6500 dollars.

❺ 未接種人數的比例突然在七月升高，讓政府官員與日俱增地感到擔憂。

_____

_____

【參考答案】

The rate of unvaccinated people skyrocketed in July, making government officials increasingly worried.

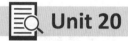

Questions 1-14 Complete the summary

The value of the Best Cinema's stocks **1.** _____ to minus 35%, causing consumer **2.** _____ to drop to the lowest point.

While the meeting offers hope to local residents, air **3.** _____ problems have been continuing to **4.** _____ since July.

The survey also concluded that water **5.** _____ would drastically deteriorate if habitat loss problems lingered.

Two major circus giants, Best Circus and ABC Circus, **6.** _____ saw an almost 9% decline and a nearly 38% surge in **7.** __ _____ over the same period.

At this point, the authorities had found **8.** _____ snake bites respectively in the mountain and the lake, implying a surge in snake numbers.

When scientists were looking for reasons for the **9.** _____ in snake numbers respectively in the river bank and mountain cliffs, they **10.** _____ found an alien species.

The price of golden four-eyed snakes **11.** _____, reaching US 60000 per kilo, a remarkable increase from 2016.

The **12.** _____ of purple octopuses skyrocketed from a low of 500 dollars to the high of 6500 dollars.

The rate of **13.** _____ people skyrocketed in July, making government officials **14.** _____ worried.

Boxes

A increasingly	**B** confidence
C pollution	**D** salinity
E respectively	**F** deteriorate
G rise	**H** deteriorated
I accidentally	**J** revenue
K skyrocketed	**L** unusual
M number	**N** unvaccinated

參考答案

1. H	2. B	3. C	4. F	5. D	6. E	7. J
8. L	9. G	10. I	11. K	12. M	13. N	14. A

Part 1

雅思百變圖表題字彙

Part 2

雅思精選小作文範文

雅思百變
圖表題字彙

Unit 21

★ 單元概述

　　第一個字彙要介紹的是 sharp，可以跟先前介紹過的 steep 輪替使用，也可以替換成 drastic, dramatic 等字彙，如果圖表中的數值有持續性顯著波動的話，還可能可以連續用上這四個字彙。第二個字彙要介紹的是 average，是個司空見慣的字彙，但是搭配百分比的部分，則較少有考生掌握到，建議可以背誦這三個例句。最後要介紹的是 ramp sth up，也是個高分的慣用語表達，且較少考生使用，不過能取代像是 enhance, increase, facilitate 等字彙，讓文章增色不少。

圖表題高分字彙 ▶ *MP3 021*

【61. sharp 突然的；急劇的；猛烈的】

Sharp

■ Uprecedented 6 million people visited Best Zoo to see marron dolphins, including foreigner visitors, a **sharp** 65.8% surge from last year.

有史無前例的 6 百萬人參訪倍斯特動物園，為了一睹紅色海豚的樣貌，包含了外國觀光客，比起去年來說有急遽的百分之六十五點八的激增。

【還能怎麼說】

■ A **sharp** drop in oxygen levels will make desert octopuses unable to survive, according to the fiction.

氧氣程度急遽下降讓沙漠章魚無法生存，根據小説。

■ A **sharp** 75% surge in the number of desert poisonous plants will cause more insect deaths, according to the fiction.

沙漠有毒植物的數量百分之七十五的激增會導致更多的昆蟲死亡，根據小説。

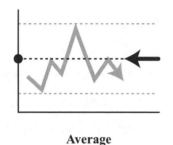

Average

【62. average 平均數是，平均為】

- The rate of decline **averaged** 25.6%, signifying a significant drop in earnings in two major hot seasons.

  下降的比率平均是百分之二十五點六，代表著在兩個主要旺季中收益有顯著的下降。

【還能怎麼說】

- Rainforest giant spiders **average** 88% more likely to pass the maze given by the researchers, and have a lower percentage of getting lured by the dead carcasses.

  在研究人員給予的迷宮，熱帶雨林巨型蜘蛛平均有百分之八十八的比率能通過，且有較低比率會受到死亡屍體的引誘。

- The rate of monkeys getting killed by eagles **averages** 36 in the region, and in less denser areas, the number is exceedingly high.

  在該地區，被老鷹殺死的猴子比率平均是 36 隻，而在較不密集的地區，數量是異常高的。

【63. ramp sth up 加快（速度）；增加（威力）；提高（費用）】

■ Best Farm has **ramped up** the production speed to meet the increasing demand of international travelers who adore tender lambs.

倍斯特農場加快了生產速度以應付喜愛柔嫩羔羊的國際旅客逐漸增加的需求量。

Ramp sth up

【還能怎麼說】

■ Widely cultivated fruits will **ramp up** the expenditure in fertilizers, but the return will be astounding.

廣泛種植的水果會迅速增加肥料的費用，但是回報卻會是驚人的。

■ To **ramp up** the fertilization of rare insect eggs, scientists are using an artificial environment that makes insects believe there is a predator nearby.

為了加快罕見昆蟲蛋的受精，科學家們正使用了人工環境，讓昆蟲相信掠食者就在附近。

185

❶ 有史無前例的 6 百萬人參訪倍斯特動物園，為了一睹紅色海豚的樣貌，包含了外國觀光客，比起去年來說有急遽的百分之六十五點八的激增。

_____

_____

【參考答案】

Unprecedented 6 million people visited Best Zoo to see marron dolphins, including foreigner visitors, a sharp 65.8% surge from last year.

❷ 在研究人員給予的迷宮，熱帶雨林巨型蜘蛛平均有百分之八十八的比率能通過，且有較低比率的會受到死亡屍體的引誘。

_____

_____

【參考答案】

Rainforest giant spiders average 88% more likely to pass the maze given by the researchers, and have a lower percentage of getting lured by the dead carcasses.

❸ 在該地區，被老鷹殺死的猴子比率平均是 36 隻，而在較不密集的地區，數量是異常高的。

_____

_____

【參考答案】
The rate of monkeys getting killed by eagles averages 36 in the region, and in less denser areas, the number is exceedingly high.

❹ 倍斯特農場加速的生產速度以應付喜愛柔嫩羔羊的國際旅客逐漸增加的需求量。

_____

_____

【參考答案】
Best Farm has ramped up the production speed to meet the increasing demand of international travelers who adore tender lambs.

❺ 為了加快罕見昆蟲蛋的受精，科學家們正使用了人工環境，讓昆蟲相信掠食者就在附近。

_____

_____

【參考答案】
To ramp up the fertilization of rare insect eggs, scientists are using an artificial environment that makes insects believe there is a predator nearby.

Questions 1-14 Complete the summary

1. _____ 6 million people visited Best Zoo to see marron dolphins, including foreigner visitors, a sharp 65.8% surge from last year.

A sharp drop in **2.** _____ levels will make desert octopuses unable to **3.** _____, according to the fiction.

A sharp 75% surge in the number of desert **4.** _____ plants will cause more insect deaths, according to the fiction.

The rate of decline **5.** _____ 25.6%, signifying a significant drop in **6.** _____ in two major hot seasons.

Rainforest giant spiders average 88% more likely to pass the maze given by the researchers, and have a lower **7.** _____ of getting lured by the dead **8.** _____.

The rate of monkeys getting killed by eagles averages 36 in the **9.** _____, and in less denser areas, the number is **10.** _____ high.

Best Farm has ramped up the production speed to meet the increasing demand of **11.** _____ travelers who **12.** _____ tender lambs.

Widely cultivated fruits will ramp up the **13.** _____ in fertilizers, but the return will be astounding.

To ramp up the **14.** _____ of rare insect eggs, scientists are using an artificial environment that makes insects believe there is a predator nearby.

Boxes

A expenditure	**B** fertilization
C exceedingly	**D** international
E earnings	**F** unprecedented
G adore	**H** carcasses
I oxygen	**J** region
K survive	**L** averaged
M percentage	**N** poisonous

參考答案

1. F	2. I	3. K	4. N	5. L	6. E	7. M
8. H	9. J	10. C	11. D	12. G	13. A	14. B

雅思百變
圖表題字彙

Unit 22

★ 單元概述

　　第一個字彙要介紹的是 total，可以跟先前介紹過的 number 輪替使用，表達總數。相關用法可以參考例句。而在第三個例句中，更用上了不同的搭配，包含 decline, on the rise 等用語，建議可以背誦起來。第二個要介紹的是高分慣用語 edge up，可以替換 have a slight increase，或是跟前面介紹過的 bulge 等輪替使用，迅速達到八分以上的高分，這三個例句都值得考生背誦。最後要介紹的是 anticipated，可以搭配百分比等，使文章表達更為靈活，第三個例句中搭配比較級的部分，更值得考生多練習。

圖表題高分字彙 ▶ *MP3 022*

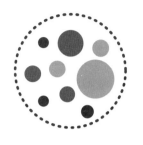

Total

【64. total 總數達；合計為】

■ Expenses for the factory maintenance **totaled** 5 million.
工廠的維護費用總計為 5 百萬用。

【還能怎麼說】

■ People getting killed by venomous plants **totaled** 50, according to the report.
根據報導，被有毒植物殺死的人總計是 50 人。

■ Numbers of zebra snakes are declining near the desert region, but the number of rattlesnakes is on the rise, **totaling** 5,589.
在鄰近沙漠地區的斑馬蛇的數量正下滑，但是響尾蛇的數量正逐漸上升，總計是 5589 條。

Edge up

【65. edge up 緩慢上升】

- Revenue for the July period **edged up** 2.9%, the sluggish growth in summer.

  七月時期的收益有緩慢的百分之二點九的爬升，在夏季中遲緩的成長。

【還能怎麼說】

- The number of seaweed collectors getting injured or killed has been **edging up** 3.9%, making the choice of being in that profession gloomy.

  海草採收員受到傷害或因而死亡的數量有百分之三點九的緩慢上升，讓選擇從事那個職業的人陰鬱。

- The surface temperature of the ocean will **edge up** a few degrees from the normal, if the emission of carbon dioxide continues to increase.

  海洋表面溫度將從正常水平緩慢上升幾度，如果二氧化碳的排放持續增加。

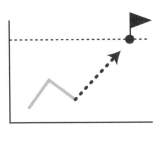

Anticipated

【 **66. anticipated** 期盼的 】

■ Revenue from giant lobsters only grew 3%, less than the **anticipated** 27%.

巨型龍蝦的收益成長了百分之三，少於原先預期的百分之二十七。

【 還能怎麼說 】

■ Despite high levels of concern about its yield, the government bond has reached the **anticipated** 25%.

儘管對於效益有高度的擔憂，政府債卷已達到了預期的百分之二十五。

■ Fruit farmers in the region contributed only 38% of the overall export, less than the **anticipated** 67%.

這個地區的水果果農僅貢獻了總出口的百分之三十八，比預期的百分之六十七更少。

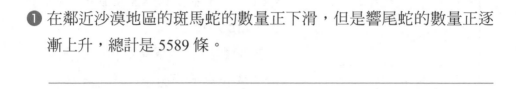

❶ 在鄰近沙漠地區的斑馬蛇的數量正下滑,但是響尾蛇的數量正逐漸上升,總計是 5589 條。

_____

_____

【參考答案】
Numbers of zebra snakes are declining near the desert region, but the number of rattlesnakes is on the rise, totaling 5,589.

❷ 七月時期的收益有緩慢的百分之二點九的爬升,在夏季中遲緩的成長。

_____

_____

【參考答案】
Revenue for the July period edged up 2.9%, the sluggish growth in summer.

❸ 海洋表面溫度將從正常水平緩慢上升幾度,如果二氧化碳的排放持續增加。

_____

_____

【參考答案】

The surface temperature of the ocean will edge up a few degrees from the normal, if the emission of carbon dioxide continues to increase.

儘管對於效益有高度的擔憂，政府債卷已達到了預期的百分之二十五。

【參考答案】

Despite high levels of concern about its yield, the government bond has reached the anticipated 25%.

這個地區的水果果農僅貢獻了總出口的百分之三十八，比預期的百分之六十七更少。

【參考答案】

Fruit farmers in the region contributed only 38% of the overall export, less than the anticipated 67%.

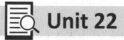

Questions 1-14 Complete the summary

Expenses for the factory **1.** _____ totaled 5 million.

People getting killed by venomous **2.** _____ totaled 50, according to the report.

Numbers of zebra snakes are **3.** _____ near the **4.** _____ region, but the number of rattlesnakes is on the rise, totaling 5,589.

Revenue for the July period edged up 2.9%, the **5.** _____ growth in summer.

The number of **6.** _____ collectors getting injured or killed has been edging up 3.9%, making the choice of being in that **7.** _____ gloomy.

The surface **8.** _____ of the ocean will edge up a few degrees from the normal, if the **9.** _____ of carbon dioxide continues to increase.

Revenue from giant lobsters only **10.** _____ 3%, less than the **11.** _____ 27%.

Despite high levels of concern about its **12.** _____, the government bond has reached the anticipated 25%.

Fruit farmers in the region **13.** _____ only 38% of the overall **14.** _____, less than the anticipated 67%.

Boxes

A emission	**B** plants
C temperature	**D** maintenance
E declining	**F** sluggish
G contributed	**H** desert
I grew	**J** profession
K anticipated	**L** seaweed
M export	**N** yield

參考答案

1. D	2. B	3. E	4. H	5. F	6. L	7. J
8. C	9. A	10. I	11. K	12. N	13. G	14. M

雅思百變
圖表題字彙

Unit 23

★ 單元概述

　　第一個字彙要介紹的是 subdued，建議可以跟前面介紹過的 sluggish 等字彙搭配使用，其搭配 growth 是很常見的表達，這點可以在例句一和三中發現。第二個介紹的是 elevenfold，也是類似於取代使用 have a dramatic increase 等字，而更具體的表達出差異，要記住它是形容詞，可以跟表動詞倍數的 double 或 triple 等輪替在不同例句中表達出數值呈現 X 倍速的差異，考生也可以使用 X times，但是沒有像 elevenfold 或 triple 等好。最後要表達的是 plateau，也是個高分字彙，可以用於表達出數值呈現出停滯，可以跟 stagnant 等字接續使用在不同例句，考生也能用類似 remain constant 這樣的表達。

圖表題高分字彙 ▶ *MP3 023*

【**67. subdued** 減弱的；減緩的】

■ **Subdued** growth of this year has made many people suffering from starvation and malnutrition.

今年減緩的成長已經導致許多人飽受飢餓和營養不良。

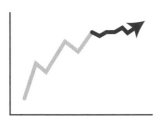

Subdued

【還能怎麼說】

■ The **subdued** tornado is still formidable and is capable of flooding the entire region.

減弱的颶風仍舊令人畏懼，且能夠讓整個地區淹沒。

■ The growth of the tech stock has become increasingly **subdued** due to a closure of several important energy plants.

由於幾間重要的能源廠的關閉，科技股的成長已經日益減緩。

【68. elevenfold 十一倍的】

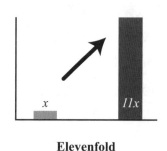

Elevenfold

- Tech stocks experienced an **elevenfold** increase, reaching 12 billion in 2019, upending conjectures made by numerous analysts.

  科技股有著 11 倍的增加，達到 2019 年的 12 億元，顛覆了為數眾多的分析師們的推測。

【還能怎麼說】

- The increasingly fierce sun has made water temperatures remarkably warmer, and an **elevenfold** increase in temperatures is able to cook all clams and lobsters in the region.

  日益猛烈的太陽已經讓水的溫度有顯著的暖化，而且溫度 11 倍的增長能夠煮熟這個地區的所有蛤蠣和龍蝦。

- The football team will get the prize that is **elevenfold** this year, making all team members thrilled.

  今年，足球隊能夠獲取 11 倍的獎酬，讓所有團隊成員都興奮異常。

【69. plateau 平穩期；停滯期】

■ The birth rate of Indian peacocks reached a **plateau** in 1960, but went through a sharp decline after the resurrection of the wild tigers.

印度孔雀的出生率在 1960 年時達到了高原期，但是在野生老虎的復甦後卻有著顯著的下滑。

Plateau

【還能怎麼說】

■ As the production has become steadier and has reached a **plateau**, managers can have more free time enjoying themselves.

隨著產量已經變得穩固且已經達到了高原期，經理能有更多的自由時間自我享受。

■ All predators will encounter the phase of a **plateau**, and after that food resources will become increasingly scarce.

所有的掠食者都會遇到高原期階段，而在那之後食物資源都會變得日益稀少。

❶ 由於幾間重要的能源廠的關閉，科技股的成長已經日益減緩。

_____

_____

【參考答案】

The growth of the tech stock has become increasingly subdued due to a closure of several important energy plants.

❷ 科技股有著 11 倍的增加，達到 2019 年的 12 億元，顛覆了為數眾多的分析師們的推測。

_____

_____

【參考答案】

Tech stocks experienced an elevenfold increase, reaching 12 billion in 2019, upending conjectures made by numerous analysts.

❸ 日益猛烈的太陽已經讓水的溫度有顯著的暖化，而且溫度 11 倍的增長能夠煮熟這個地區的所有蛤蠣和龍蝦。

_____

_____

【參考答案】
The increasingly fierce sun has made water temperatures remarkably warmer, and an elevenfold increase in temperatures is able to cook all clams and lobsters in the region.

❹ 印度孔雀的出生率在 1960 年時達到了高原期，但是在野生老虎的復甦後卻有著顯著的下滑。

_____

_____

【參考答案】
The birth rate of Indian peacocks reached a plateau in 1960, but went through a sharp decline after the resurrection of the wild tigers.

❺ 所有的掠食者都會遇到高原期階段，而在那之後食物資源都會變得日益稀少。

_____

_____

【參考答案】
All predators will encounter the phase of a plateau, and after that food resources will become increasingly scarce.

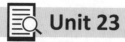

Unit 23

Questions 1-14 Complete the summary

Subdued growth of this year has made many people suffering from starvation and **1.** _____.

The subdued tornado is still **2.** _____ and is capable of flooding the entire region.

The growth of the tech stock has become increasingly **3.** _____ _____ due to a **4.** _____ of several important energy plants.

Tech stocks experienced an **5.** _____ increase, reaching 12 billion in 2019, upending **6.** _____ made by numerous analysts.

The increasingly fierce sun has made water temperatures **7.** __ _____ warmer, and an elevenfold increase in temperatures is able to **8.** _____ all clams and lobsters in the region.

The football team will get the prize that is elevenfold this year, making all team members **9.** _____.

The birth rate of Indian peacocks reached a **10.** _____ in 1960, but went through a sharp decline after the **11.** _____ _____ of the wild tigers.

As the production has become **12.** _____ and has reached a plateau, managers can have more free time enjoying themselves.

All **13.** _____ will encounter the phase of a plateau, and after that food resources will become increasingly **14.** ___ _____.

Boxes

A plateau	**B** resurrection
C formidable	**D** subdued
E cook	**F** closure
G steadier	**H** thrilled
I scarce	**J** remarkably
K predators	**L** elevenfold
M conjectures	**N** malnutrition

參考答案

1. N	2. C	3. D	4. F	5. L	6. M	7. J
8. E	9. H	10. A	11. B	12. G	13. K	14. I

UNIT 01　雙表格題：
萬能藥水和其效用

Writing Task 1

You should spend about 20 minutes on this task

The diagram below includes two tables: table a and table b. Table a contains information about magic potions during the clinical trials, whereas table b is made up of magic potions on the market.

Analyze effects, duration, side effects, costs, and failure rates of magic potions. Make a comparison about figures and percentages listed in the table. You can also make an inference about the future trend that effects of these magic potions on current lifestyles of modern human beings.

Write at least 150 words

206

整合能力強化 ❶ 實際演練

請搭配左頁的題目和下方的圖片進行圖表題寫作的演練。

Table a： during clinical trials

Magic portions

items	failure rates	Side effects	Rates of SE
Wisdom	20%	anorexia, weight gain	20%
Memory	20%	anorexia, asthma	20%
Power	50%	dyslexia, hypertension	20%
Muscle-building	50%	dyslexia, leukemia	20%
Cancer-free	80%	anemia, memory loss	80%
Love	80%	weight gain	80%

Table b： on the market

Magic portions

items	effects	duration	costs
Fly	Flying ability	a day	US 1,000
Wisdom	super smart	perpetual	US 50,000
Memory	excellent memory	eternal	US 50,000
Power	Incredible strength	temporary	US 3,000
Youth	A year younger	lasting	US 99,999
Muscle-building	Can be instantly American Captain-like	eternal	US 10,000
Cancer-free	Immunity	perpetual	US 99,999
Love	love	eternal	US 20,000

❶ 值得注意的是，飛行藥水的花費僅是肌肉建造藥水花費的十分之一，而快速掃視兩種表格可以察覺出飛行藥水並沒有任何的副作用。

_____

_____

【參考答案】

Also noteworthy is the fact that the cost of flying potions takes only one-tenth than that of the muscle-building potions, and a quick glance at both tables can reveal the fact that flying potions did not have any side effects.

❷ 儘管如此，青春藥水在臨床試驗期間並沒有任何的副作用存在且它們的效用能維持永久。

_____

_____

【參考答案】

Nevertheless, youth potions also did not have any side effects during the clinical trials and their capacity can be forever.

整合能力強化 ❸ 段落拓展

TOPIC

The diagram below includes two tables: table a and table b. Table a contains information about magic potions during the clinical trials, whereas table b is made up of magic potions on the market.

Analyze effects, duration, side effects, costs, and failure rates of magic potions. Make a comparison about figures and percentages listed in the table. You can also make the inference about the future trend that effects of these magic potions on current lifestyles of modern human beings.

Step 1   先看題目的圖表題為何種形式，並統一以 **Given is/ are**…**diagram(s)**…或 **A glance at the graph(s)**…等套句開頭，避免使用 the pic shows…等較低階的簡單句型。

Step 2   題目中包含了兩個圖表，可以立即運用兩個圖表間的差異和相似性做出比較。關於這些比較，可以參考範文中的表達（包含運用價格差異等）。考生也可以選取其他項目當作開頭。

Step 3   另外一個部分是，哪些魔法藥水是沒有副作用的，可以針對這點在飛行藥水等部分著墨其差異性。也要注意比較級的使用，這篇運用了很多這類的表達，如果在這部份很弱的考生，可以背誦此篇，提升自己寫這方面句型時的敏銳度。這部份其實要追溯回國中的代名詞指代等的用法。使用比較級時，兩個名詞或兩名詞片語要是能比較的對象，否則就會造成比較對象不一致。對此，考生可以仔細檢視文句中有that of/those of 等的表達句，並多注意寫作文劇中兩個比較對象。

Step 4   最後要說明的是敘事手法，考生可以分別介紹後再總結，也能採取其他策略。但還有一點是，範文中進行推論的部分，關於這點可以藉由表格中的數值去思考出或反推出某個能力藥水的上市是否會影響某個未來產業或趨勢，並藉由這部分進一步深入表達。

整合能力強化 ❹ 參考範文 ▶ *MP3 024*

經由先前的演練後，現在請看整篇範文並聆聽音檔

Given are two tables about magic potions during the clinical trials and on the market. In Table a, failure rates of wisdom potions and memory potions stood at 20%, though side effects of both potions were slightly different. Both exhibited the symptom of anorexia, but wisdom potions came at the cost of having weight gain. In power potions and muscle building potions, failure rates were equivalent. Side effects included difficulty in learning to read, and had pathological changes in blood vessels. It is intriguing to note that love potions had the identical side effect as the wisdom potions. That meant a change in physical appearance was the price to pay for using love potions and wisdom potions. However, in love potions, the chance of getting overweight was a startling 80%, four times as high as that of the wisdom potions.

提供的兩個表格圖是關於在臨床試驗期間和上市後的魔法藥水。在 Table a，智慧藥水和記憶藥水的失敗率是 20%，儘管兩種藥水的副作用有些許的不同。兩者均顯示了厭食症的症狀，但是智慧藥水還要付出的代價是體重增加。在力量藥水和肌肉建造的藥水中，兩者的失敗率是相同的。副作用包含了閱讀學習上的困難，而且在血管中均有病變發生。引人注目的是，愛

情藥水跟智慧藥水有同樣的副作用。那也意謂著使用愛情藥水和智慧藥水所要付出的代價是外表的改變。然而，在愛情藥水中，有驚人的百分之八十的機率使體重增加，為智慧藥水副作用的四倍。

In Table b, the price for youth potions and cancer-free potions are the highest, almost thirty-three times expensive than that of the power potions. From the information supplied, the duration of both youth potions and cancer-free potions are eternal, whereas the power potions are transient. That is, a noticeable boost in strength will not be forever. Also noteworthy is the fact that the cost of flying potions takes only one-tenth than that of the muscle-building potions, and a quick glance at both tables can reveal the fact that flying potions did not have any side effects. The reason might be because of its duration lasts only for a day, while other potions can have an eternal efficacy. Nevertheless, youth potions also did not have any side effects during the clinical trials and their capacity can be forever.

在 Table b，青春藥水和免於癌症的藥水的價格是最高昂的，幾乎是力量藥水價格的 33 倍。從所提供的資訊顯示，青春藥水和免於癌症的藥水的效期是永久的，而力量藥水的效期是短暫的。也就是說，力量的顯著增加無法持久。值得注意的是，飛行藥水的花費僅是肌肉建造藥水花費的十分之一，而快速掃視兩種表格可以察覺出飛行藥水並沒有任何的副作用。原因可能是因為其效用僅維持一天，而其他藥水卻有永久的效用。儘管

如此，青春藥水在臨床試驗期間並沒有任何的副作用存在且它們的效用能維持永久。

Other than the above-mentioned comparisons, inferences can be drawn about all these magic potions. With the development of these magic potions, it is likely that in the future the number of gym users will be significantly dwindled. With cancer-free potions getting widespread, there is going to be an exceedingly high likelihood that the expertise of cancer treatment doctors will be worthless. Lastly, people taking love potions will create a new phenomenon that noticeably reduces the number of single parents.

除了上述所提到的比較之外，從這些魔法藥水中也能做出推論。隨著這些魔法藥水的進展，很可能在未來使用健身房的人數將會顯著減少。隨著免於癌症的藥水更廣於流傳，治療癌症醫生的專業變得不具價值是有極高的可能性。最後，服用愛情藥水的人也會產生一個新的現象，而顯著地減低了單身父母的數量。

UNIT
02
雙表格題：
新冠疫情時事題

 Writing Task 1

You should spend about 20 minutes on this task

The diagram below includes two tables: table a and table b. Table a contains four major components related to COVID-19, whereas table b includes other information about COVID-19.

Compare and contrast about past situations in six countries and help readers get the general information by using these figures.

Write at least 150 words

整合能力強化 ❶ 實際演練

請搭配左頁的題目和下方的圖片進行圖表題寫作的演練。

Table a：COVID 19/2021/11/30

country	social distancing	lockdown	cases (wave/surging)	herd immunity threshold
A	increased	full/7/175 days	third wave	75%
B	diminished	partial/2/50 days	second wave	45%
C	enlarged	total/5/160 days	third wave	85%
D	enlarged	full/6/150 days	third wave	80%
E	decreased	partial/3/50 days	second wave	60%
F	reduced	partial/1/20 days	first wave	45%

Table b：COVID 19/2021/11/30

country	reinfection rate	age 6-12	unvaccinated adults	Deaths driven by
A	62%	eligible	40%	delta
B	60%	unqualified	80%	omicron
C	55%	eligible	35%	delta
D	58%	ineligible	45%	delta
E	56%	qualified	70%	omicron
F	55%	unqualified	70%	omicron

❶ 在 Table a，疫情期間，Country A 具有 7 次的完全封鎖，總計達 175 天，為世界上任何國家中封鎖日期最長的，而 Country F 卻有最少次數的封鎖，有著社交距離的減少和部分封鎖。

_____

_____

【參考答案】

In Table a, Country A had 7 full lockdowns during the pandemic, summing up 175 days, the most of any country in the world, whereas Country F had the least lockdown and was left with reduced social distancing, partial lockdown.

❷ 從所提供的資訊顯示，在六個國家中，Country F 過去是唯一一個仍只有第一波疫情的國家，而其他國家卻顯示出案例激增且有超過一波的疫情。

_____

_____

【參考答案】

From the information supplied, Country F was the only one still in the first wave among all six countries, while others exhibited surging in cases for more than once.

❸ 為了抑制進一步的疫情爆發，新冠疫情的群體免疫門檻可能與擴大的社交距離和完全封鎖有高度的相關。

_____

_____

【參考答案】

To curb the further outbreak, the covid-19 herd immunity threshold might be highly related to enlarged social distancing and full lockdowns.

❹ 也值得注意的是，新的變異株 omicron 的威脅讓人們感到擔憂。

_____

_____

【參考答案】

Also remarkable is the fact that the new variant omicron's threat made people concerned.

❺ 總結來說，儘管不同的國家經歷著不同樣的案例激增和死亡，不論是由 delta 或是 omicron 引起的，再次感染率均維持恆定，擺動於百分之五十五與六十二之間。

_____

_____

【參考答案】

In conclusion, despite the fact that different countries were encountering different surging in cases and death driven by either delta or omicron, reinfection rates remained constant, vacillating between 55％ to 62％.

TOPIC

The diagram below includes two tables: table a and table b. Table a contains four major components related to COVID-19, whereas table b includes other information about COVID-19.

Compare and contrast about past situations in six countries and help readers get the general information by using these figures.

Step 1　先看題目的圖表題為何種形式，並統一以 **Given is/ are**…**diagram(s)**…或 **A glance at the graph(s)**…等套句開頭，避免使用 the pic shows…等較低階的簡單句型。

Step 2　這題也結合了時事且為鑑別度高的一題。因為搭配了許多疫情相關的字彙和數值後，要描述得很順暢其實不太容易。關於這點可以參照段落的各種表達。另外，考生也可以針對以下這八點 social distancing/lockdown/cases/ herd immunity threshold/ reinfection rate/age 6-12/unvaccinated adults/Deaths driven by（delta or omicron），來進行描寫和

分析或比較，不一定要照範文的表達，針對不同分析特點亦能剖析出不一樣的高分範文。

Step 3　以描述手法來說，可以分別介紹兩個圖表，最後再總結出訊息。也能改採用不同的敘述方式，例如直接比較出兩個圖表中的異同和各個國家之間的差異或相似處。文章中也可以適時增添一些訊息，例如「首段的 Country F 的居民在日常活動中有較少的限制。」

Step 4　最後要注意的是，在運用比較級的時候要注意修辭方面的使用，名詞片語之間的比較，要看前方主要名詞，最後加上 than that of...或 than those of...，這部分也影響到關鍵得分。

經由先前的演練後，現在請看整篇範文並聆聽音檔

Given are two tables about covid-19 and its myriad features in six countries. In Table a, Country A had 7 full lockdowns during the pandemic, summing up 175 days, the most of any country in the world, whereas Country F had the least lockdown and was left with reduced social distancing, partial lockdown. It can be inferred that residents of Country F were having less constraints on daily activities.

提供的是關於六個國家中新冠肺炎和其多樣特徵的兩個圖表。在 Table a，疫情期間，Country A 具有 7 次的完全封鎖，總計達 175 天，為世界上任何國家中封鎖日期最長的，而 Country F 卻有最少次數的封鎖，有著社交距離的減少和部分封鎖。也能推測出，Country F 的居民在日常活動中有較少的限制。

From the information supplied, Country F was the only one still in the first wave among all six countries, while others exhibited surging in cases for more than once. Due to its light condition, Country B and Country F's herd immunity threshold were respectively set on only 45%, significantly lower than that of Country A's 75% and Country C's 85%. To curb the further outbreak, the covid-19 herd immunity threshold might be highly related to enlarged social distancing and full lockdowns.

從所提供的資訊顯示，在六個國家中，Country F 過去是唯一一個仍只有第一波疫情的國家，而其他國家卻顯示出案例激增且有超過一波的疫情。由於其輕微的情況，Country B 和 Country F 的群體免疫門檻分別僅設在 45％，比起 Country A 的 75％和 Country C 的 85％，比例顯然更低。為了抑制進一步的疫情爆發，新冠疫情的群體免疫門檻可能與擴大的社交距離和完全封鎖有高度的相關。

Also remarkable is the fact that the new variant omicron's threat made people concerned. In Table b, three countries had found traces of omicron even with a more tightening policy. Along with the track of the new variant, deaths were accompanied by its presence. The highest reinfection rate was seen in Country A. Two of them had reinfection rates over 60％ as of 30 November. Overall, even with the appearance of omicron, reinfection rates fluctuated between 55％ to 62％.

也值得注意的是，新的變異株 omicron 的威脅讓人們感到擔憂。在 Table b，即使採取了更加嚴格的政策，三個國家都發現了 omicron 的蹤跡，且死亡伴隨著此病毒的現蹤。在 Country A 有著最高的再次感染率。到 11 月 30 日為止，其中的兩個國家的再次感染率都超過了 60％。整體來說，即使隨著 omicron 的出現，再次感染率在 55％到 62％間波動。

In Country A, 60％ of adults have been vaccinated. It is intriguing to note that countries that exhibited presence of omicron were having over 70％ of unvaccinated adults, whereas countries' deaths driven by delta had less than 45％ of unvaccinated adults. In some countries, children aged 6-12 were allowed to get the jab, but that did not have any correlation with reinfection rates and deaths driven by omicron.

在 Country A，60％的成人都已接種疫苗了。引人注目的是，有顯示出 omicron 的蹤跡的國家有超過 70％的成人尚未接種疫苗，而由 delta 所引起的死亡的國家有著少於 45％的成人尚未接種疫苗。在有些國家中，年紀介於 6-12 歲的小孩允許接種疫苗，但是那與由 omicron 所引起的再次感染率和死亡並沒有任何的關聯性。

In conclusion, despite the fact that different countries were encountering different surging in cases and death driven by either delta or omicron, reinfection rates remained constant, vacillating between 55％ to 62％. As can be seen in Table b, focusing on the unvaccinated adults might be the key to counter with the invasion of omicron. However, it remains to be seen whether an increase in adult vaccinations and age of children eligible for the injection will be the stop to new variants.

總結來說，儘管不同的國家經歷著不同的案例激增和死亡，不論是由 delta 或是 omicron 引起的，再次感染率均維持恆定，擺

動於 55％至 62％之間。如 Table b 所示，重點放在未接種的成人可能是應對 omicron 侵略的關鍵點。然而，成人接種的增加和小孩合乎注射資格的年紀是否將能阻擋新的病毒變異尚未被預測出。

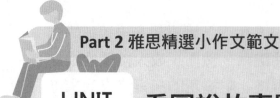

UNIT 03

看圖說故事題：

螃蟹和章魚

📖 Writing Task 1

You should spend about 20 minutes on this task

You will see four graphs with different scenarios. It was about a normal day on the shoal. On the surface, there were beautiful scenes carved out the natural wonders, but deep down dangers were everywhere. Things could always change in a blink of an eye. What would happen to the crab?

Describe four scenarios in details by listed graphs. Use your imagination and creativity when necessary to complete the whole narrative.

Write at least 150 words

整合能力強化 ❶ 實際演練

請搭配左頁的題目和下方的圖片進行圖表題寫作的演練。

Shoal A

Shoal B

Shoal C

Shoal D

Part 2
雅思精選小作文範文

❶ 在寧靜美麗的淺灘上，一隻有著一對巨大螯足的螃蟹似乎輕鬆自
在，但卻又保持警覺。

【參考答案】

On a serene beautiful shoal, a crab with a pair of large pincers
seemed relaxed but remained cautious.

❷ 在礁岩上的水是清澈透明的，而偶爾螃蟹會製造幾個泡泡讓自己
的口部保持濕潤。

【參考答案】

The water on the coral knoll was transparent, and once in a while,
the crab created a few bubbles to keep its mouth moist.

❸ 螃蟹快速地移動至下一個大型礁岩處，躲避那些章魚觸手的攻
擊。隨著螃蟹和章魚追逐的展開，緊張感也與日俱增。

【參考答案】

The crab swiftly moved to the next large knoll, dodging the attack of those tentacles of octopuses. The tension was mounting as the chase between the crab and octopus had begun.

❹ 章魚無法抗拒這樣的美食，所以牠又進行了幾次行動以擄住螃蟹。

_____

_____

【參考答案】

The octopus could not resist the delicious meal, so it made a few more attempts to grab the crab.

❺ 章魚興高采烈地帶走這個大餐沉到水裡去了，且準備享用大餐。

_____

_____

【參考答案】

The octopus gleefully took the meal sinking into the water, and ready to have a great meal.

TOPIC

You will see four graphs with different scenarios. It was about a normal day on the shoal. On the surface, there were beautiful scenes carved out the natural wonders, but deep down dangers were everywhere. Things could always change in a blink of an eye. What would happen to the crab?

Describe four scenarios in details by listed graphs. Use your imagination and creativity when necessary to complete the whole narrative.

Step 1　先看題目的圖表題為何種形式，並統一以 **Given is/ are**...**diagram(s)**...或 **A glance at the graph(s)**...等套句開頭，避免使用 the pic shows...等較低階的簡單句型。

Step 2　首段中就很考驗說故事能力，先鋪陳和描述背景後，慢慢帶出這張圖的核心故事，以及螃蟹的動作。當中還包含了描述到螃蟹的巨大螯足等細節性資訊。這點在雅思考試中至關重要。因為描述的是否具體是獲取寫作 7 分以上成績的關鍵。

Step 3　　接著，運用敘述和說故事能力完成接下來的三張圖表。章魚的潛伏和行動以及螃蟹並未意識到危險等均為一項好的發揮特點。此外也能著墨在，兩者間的攻防，以及螃蟹如何避開章魚觸手或是找尋礁岩做掩蔽等增加其生動性。最後，描述螃蟹難逃死劫和成為章魚的大餐，完成這篇作文。

Step 4　　時態的部分，全篇都是使用過去式描述，因為發生在過去的一段時間。另外一個重點是關於一些字彙的掌握，像是章魚的觸手等的英文單字都會連帶影響到表達，運用 tentacles 一定比使用 hands 或更模糊的表達來得好。還有其他細節性的描述和形容詞等，例如 bulging 等，可以參考範文。

經由先前的演練後，現在請看整篇範文並聆聽音檔

Shoal A

On a serene beautiful shoal, a crab with a pair of large pincers seemed relaxed but remained cautious. The water in the coral knoll was transparent, and once in a while, the crab created plenty of bubbles to keep its mouth moist. Then it moved sideways towards the water, and felt great about getting itself watery.

在寧靜美麗的淺灘上，一隻有著一對巨大螯足的螃蟹似乎輕鬆自在，但卻又保持警覺。在礁岩上的水是清澈透明的，而偶爾螃蟹會製造大量的泡泡讓自己的口部保持濕潤。緊接著，牠側著走向水裡，對於讓自己身體浸濕感到舒暢。

Shoal B

As it walked and tried to search for something to eat, an exceedingly large octopus lurked near the place where the crab stood. As can be seen from the graph, the octopus only revealed its head and two bulging eyes above the water. The crab was still unaware of the danger until the movement of the octopus scared it.

隨著牠行走並且試著找尋食物來吃，一隻異常巨大的章魚潛伏在靠近螃蟹所待的地方。如圖所示，章魚僅將自己的頭部和兩隻張大的眼睛留在水位上方。螃蟹仍然沒有察覺到危險，直到章魚的動作驚嚇到牠。

Shoal C

The crab swiftly moved to the next large knoll, dodging the attack of those tentacles of octopuses. The tension was mounting as the chase between the crab and octopus had begun. The octopus could not resist the delicious meal, so it made a few more attempts to grab the crab.

螃蟹快速地移動至下一個大型礁岩處，躲避那些章魚觸手的攻擊。隨著螃蟹和章魚追逐的展開，緊張感也與日俱增。章魚無法抗拒這樣的美食，所以牠又進行了幾次行動以攫住螃蟹。

Shoal D

Those tentacles were not that easy to get rid of, and the next moment the crab had several struggles. It was in the arms of the octopus, and its fate was inevitable. The octopus gleefully took the meal sinking into the water, and ready to have a great meal.

那些觸手並不是那麼容易擺脫，在下個時刻螃蟹有幾次的掙扎。牠已經身處章魚的臂膀之間，命數已定了。章魚興高采烈地帶走這個大餐沉到水裡去了，且準備享用大餐。

UNIT 04

看圖說故事題：

北極熊現在攻擊馴鹿了嗎？

 Writing Task 1

You should spend about 20 minutes on this task

Four graphs list an unusual phenomenon in the Arctic. Polar bears have changed their feeding habits from hunting seal cubs to reindeers. It is highly unlikely, but it is actually happening due to global warming and other factors.

Use your imagination and creativity by combining four drawings with the news. Your storytelling techniques will be graded.

Write at least 150 words

整合能力強化 ❶ 實際演練

請搭配左頁的題目和下方的圖片進行圖表題寫作的演練。

Graph A

Graph B

Graph C

Graph D

Part 2

雅思精選小作文範文

233

❶ 牠們能夠在遠處就察覺到海豹寶寶的蹤跡，但是北極熊確實需要挖掘雪地以捕到海豹寶寶，此舉讓海豹寶寶有足夠的時間逃走。

_____

_____

【參考答案】

They can detect the trace of seal cubs from a distance, but polar bears do need to dig up the snow to get the cub, which gives the seal cub enough time to escape.

❷ 毛上紅通通的似乎讓牠生氣蓬勃，就像是一幅很棒的白色畫上有著紅色的點綴而讓其熠熠生輝。

_____

_____

【參考答案】

The reddening fur seems to give it vivacity, like a great white painting with the red to make it alive.

❸ 在夏季，退去的海冰已經讓捕獲海豹變得困難。

_____

_____

【參考答案】

In summer, receding sea ice has made hunting seals difficult.

整合能力強化 ❸ 段落拓展

TOPIC

Four graphs list an unusual phenomenon in the Arctic. Polar bears have changed their feeding habits from seal cubs to reindeers. It is highly unlikely, but it is actually happening due to global warming and other factors.

Use your imagination and creativity by combining four drawings with the news. Your storytelling techniques will be graded.

Step 1　先看題目的圖表題為何種形式，並統一以 **Given is/ are**...**diagram(s)**...或 **A glance at the graph(s)**...等套句開頭，避免使用 the pic shows...等較低階的簡單句型。

Step 2　這篇結合了時事且非常生活化。除了照所看到的四張圖描述外，也能增加一些自己的想像力在上頭，首段就包含了描述北極熊的習性以及其和海豹之間的關係進一步加以描述，而雖然圖表部分不是彩色的，但仍可以在腦海中預想到，北極熊吃海豹時的畫面，血液會濺到或沾染到北極熊潔白的毛上頭，而寫出更生動的描述。關於這點考生可以看第二段範文的表達。

Step 3　接著描述到這些轉變並結合新聞時事，並如圖示描述出冰山的融化使得北極熊沒有食物可供食用，導致這些轉變。再來也是需要一些說故事能力，包含北極熊和馴鹿之間的互動，掠食者和被捕食者的關係等，段落敘述中就包含了像是將失去冷靜和強而有力的攻擊等加到描述的語句中。最後描述北極熊享用馴鹿的部分。

Step 4　而關於時態和句型表達，可以參考範文的表達。當中也必須要適時使用一些較難的生字以獲取更高的成績。

整合能力強化 ④ 參考範文 ▶ *MP3 027*

經由先前的演練後，現在請看整篇範文並聆聽音檔

Graph A

Seal cubs are usually hidden beneath the snow to avoid the danger from predators, such as polar bears. Polar bears are known for its acute sense of smell. They can detect the trace of seal cubs from a distance, but polar bears do need to dig up the snow to get the cub, which gives the seal cub enough time to escape. The chance for getting the meal is slim, around 1/20, but polar bears do need the heavy fat from seal meat to survive the harsh environment.

海豹寶寶通常藏匿在雪下方以躲避掠食者，例如北極熊的威脅。北極熊以其敏銳的嗅覺而聞名。牠們能夠在遠處就察覺到海豹寶寶的蹤跡，但是北極熊確實需要挖掘雪地以捕到海豹寶寶，此舉讓海豹寶寶有足夠的時間逃走。捕獲這樣的海豹肉的機會是微乎其微的，大約是二十分之一，但是北極熊確實需要海豹肉上的厚重脂肪以生存於嚴酷的環境裡。

As can be seen from the graph, a polar bear which successfully hunts the seal, will instantly gets its nose and fur with blood. The reddening fur seems to give it vivacity, like a great white painting with the red to make it alive. It is a great thing for the bear, but unlucky for those seals which get found.

如圖所示，成功捕獲海豹的北極熊立即讓自己的鼻子和毛沾到血液。毛上紅通通的似乎讓牠生氣蓬勃，就像是一幅很棒的白色畫上有著紅色的點綴而讓其摺摺生輝。這對北極熊來說是件好事，但是對那些被找到的海豹來說卻是不幸。

Graph B

Now things seem to have changed. A recent news report revealed that polar bears have changed their diet from seals to caribous. In summer, receding sea ice has made hunting seals difficult. They are far less likely to survive if there is not enough food to eat.

現在事情似乎有了轉變。近期一則新聞報導揭露了北極熊飲食習慣從海豹轉變成馴鹿。在夏季，退去的海冰已經讓捕獲海豹變得困難。如果沒有充足的食物可供食用，北極熊極不可能存活下去。

Graph C

As can be seen from the graph, a reindeer is getting chased by a polar bear even though the reindeer can run faster. However, during the chase, the reindeer is not aware that it gets chased towards a cold ocean. As the polar bear is gradually getting near, the reindeer is panic, losing the coolness to run to the right direction. The polar bear is launching a powerful attack that makes the reindeer sink into the ocean. The polar bear happily makes a jump towards the prey and with its claws touching the caribou body. In a few seconds, the heavy weight of the polar bear makes the prey easily getting dragged down.

如圖所示，北極熊正在追逐一頭馴鹿，即使馴鹿能跑得更快。然而，在追逐期間，馴鹿並未察覺到自己被朝著冰冷的海洋方向追逐。當北極熊逐步靠近時，馴鹿慌了，失去了跑回正確方向的冷靜。北極熊發起了強而有力的攻擊，讓馴鹿沉到了海裡。北極熊雀躍地躍向獵物，以其爪子觸及馴鹿身體。幾秒內，北極熊沉重的身軀將獵物輕而易舉地往下拖。

Graph D

The polar bear is now enjoying the victory and has been gluttonously eating the caribou to store enough nutrients.

北極熊正在岸邊享受勝利的成果，且狼吞虎嚥地吃著馴鹿以儲備足夠的營養。

UNIT 05 地圖題：
倍斯特島嶼的藏寶圖

 Writing Task 1

You should spend about 20 minutes on this task

The diagram is the map of Best Island that includes three caves and other components. In these caves, treasure hunters will get the information they need to get plenty of gold, but they have to get to the destination.

Describe three caves in details. You can list information you see on the map or make a comparison about three caves and their surroundings.

Write at least 150 words

整合能力強化 **❶** 實際演練

請搭配左頁的題目和下方的圖片進行圖表題寫作的演練。

❶ 第二個洞穴靠近能頻繁看見野生動物的河岸。

_____

_____

【參考答案】

The second is near the river bank where wild animals can be frequently seen.

❷ 要抵達第三個洞穴必須要跋涉乾燥的沙漠以抵達目的地。

_____

_____

【參考答案】

To get to the third cave, one has to traverse an arid desert to get there.

❸ 該地區的動物遷徙相當頻繁,使得這個地區不適宜前往。

_____

_____

【參考答案】

Animal migrations are quite frequent in the area which make it a not ideal place to go.

❹ 賞金獵人需要前往東方的遊牧部落以獲取機動性極佳的駱駝，否則，長途跋涉到第三個洞穴的位置頗為蒸沙為飯的。

_____

_____

【參考答案】

Treasure hunters do need to go to the north east (nomadic tribe) to get camels with great mobility; otherwise, journey through a long distance to get to the location of the third cave is quite unlikely.

❺ 然而，賞金獵人必須要抵達山崖處，位於極北之地以獲取罕見花朵，才能免於蜂螫。

_____

_____

【參考答案】

However, treasure hunters have to arrive at the cliff, which is located in extreme north, to get the rare flowers to be immune from bee stings.

TOPIC

The diagram is the map of Best Island that includes three caves and other components. In these caves, treasure hunters will get the information they need to get plenty of gold, but they have to get to the destination.

Describe three caves in details. You can list information you see on the map or make a comparison about three caves and their surroundings.

Step 1　先看題目的圖表題為何種形式，並統一以 **Given is/ are...diagram(s)**...或 **A glance at the graph(s)**...等套句開頭，避免使用 the pic shows...等較低階的簡單句型。

Step 2　不知道要如何開頭的話，可以使用 from the information supplied... or also remarkable is the fact that...等句型協助描述。可以先看地圖上的三個主要描述點，即三個洞穴，並先開始簡單描述出三個洞穴之間不同的特點，周遭有什麼物品等等，可以一一列出。

Step 3　運用地圖的方位，表達出這幾個洞穴的位置，可以試著構
思出跟範文不一樣的回答，用相對位置等的概念去描述出
三個洞穴和其他地圖上的特點。例如，這個洞穴的位置在
第一個洞穴的反方向，而非直接說出該洞穴是位於東方。

Step 4　除了比較三個洞穴的特點之外，描述時，仍要加上一些創
意和敘事能力，讓文章更順暢，例如加上賞金獵人可能需
要到某個地點以獲取駱駝，或是指出某個相似或相異點，
例如在文末就有「引人注目的是，在鄰近這些洞穴的地方
都有蜂巢」這樣的表達。

經由先前的演練後，現在請看整篇範文並聆聽音檔

There are three caves on Best Island. Each with its unique covering. The first cave is in a dense forest that can be hard to detect. The second is near the river bank where wild animals can be frequently seen. To get to the third cave, one has to traverse an arid desert to get there.

在倍斯特島嶼上有三個洞穴。每個洞穴均有其獨特的遮蔽。第一個洞穴身處茂密的森林，很難察覺。第二個洞穴靠近能頻繁看見野生動物的河岸。要抵達第三個洞穴必須要跋涉乾燥的沙漠以抵達目的地。

From the information supplied, the first cave is in the west and it is humid. Rainfall is remarkably massive, so flooding is a common scene. As for the second cave, animals can be a hindrance to get closer to the cave. Animal migrations are quite frequent in the area which makes it a not ideal place to go. Its location is in the opposite direction of the first cave. The third one is in the south where camels are exceedingly rare. Treasure hunters do need to go to the north east (nomadic tribe) to get camels with great mobility; otherwise, journey through a long distance to get to the location of the third cave is quite unlikely.

從所提供的資訊可看出，第一個洞穴位於西方且是潮濕的。降雨量顯著地大，所以水災是常見的景象。至於第二個洞穴，動物可能是接近該洞穴的阻礙。該地區的動物遷徙相當頻繁，使得這個地區不適宜前往。這個洞穴的位置在第一個洞穴的反方向（東方）。第三個洞穴位於南方，也是駱駝極為罕見之地。賞金獵人需要前往東北方的遊牧部落以獲取機動性極佳的駱駝，否則，長途跋涉到第三個洞穴的位置頗為蒸沙為飯的。

It is also intriguing to note that there are beehives neighboring these caves, which can be the proof that the exact location is adjacent. However, treasure hunters have to arrive at the cliff, which is located in extreme north, to get the rare flowers to be immune from bee stings.

引人注目的是，在鄰近這些洞穴的地方都有蜂巢，也能成為判定確切位置就在附近的證據。然而，賞金獵人必須要抵達山崖處，位於極北之地以獲取罕見花朵，才能免於蜂螫。

UNIT 06 流程圖題：
韓式泡菜製作流程

 Writing Task 1

You should spend about 20 minutes on this task

The diagram below includes seven procedures about making the simple Korean kimchi. Describe these procedures in order and make them easily understandable.

The sequence is the key. Using these graphs while composing the article. You can add your knowledge about the dish to make it more appealing.

Write at least 150 words

整合能力強化 ❶ 實際演練

請搭配左頁的題目和下方的圖片進行圖表題寫作的演練。

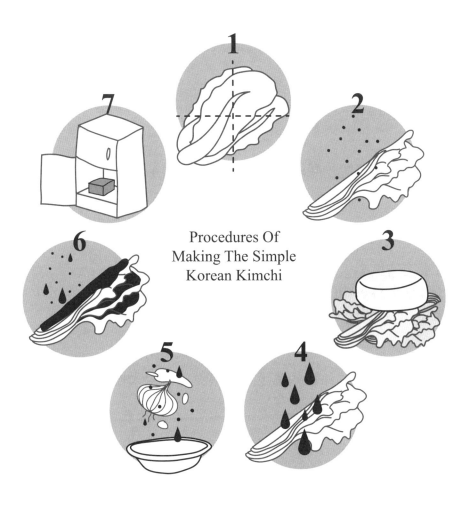

Procedures Of
Making The Simple
Korean Kimchi

❶ 製作這道享譽盛名的菜餚包含了七個步驟。

_____

_____

【參考答案】

Seven steps are included for making this prestigious dish.

❷ 鹽是大白菜發酵的關鍵，必將鹽均勻灑在白菜葉上。

_____

_____

【參考答案】

Salt is the key in the fermentation of the cabbage and sprinkle salt onto the cabbage leaves equally.

❸ 第四個步驟是移除這些葉子上的鹽份，使得大白菜能維持無鹽且可供食用。

_____

_____

【參考答案】

The fourth step is about removal of salt on these leaves and the cabbage can remain not salty and edible.

❹ 這些成分是由紅辣椒、洋蔥、大蒜和魚露所組成的。

_____

_____

【參考答案】

These ingredients are made up of red pepper, an onion, garlic, and fish sauce.

❺ 將糊均勻分布在大白菜葉子上直到葉子都浸泡出風味。

_____

_____

【參考答案】

Spreading the paste evenly onto the cabbage leaves until they are soaked with flavor.

TOPIC

The diagram below includes seven procedures about making the simple Korean kimchi. Describe these procedures in order and make them easily understandable.

The sequence is the key. Using these graphs while composing the article. You can add your knowledge about the dish to make it more appealing.

Step 1 先看題目的圖表題為何種形式，並統一以 **Given is/ are**...diagram(s)...或 **A glance at the graph(s)**...等套句開頭，避免使用 the pic shows...等較低階的簡單句型。

Step 2 可以增添一些變化，不一定要照 listing patterns 描述（即第一步驟到第七步驟），例如在段落中有使用到 **the next step**...和 **final step**...都是另一種替換。

Step 3 另一部分是，如作文中也有提到的就是使用你對於這道菜餚的知識，增進表達。在首段就包含了煮菜經驗的部分並

適時融入步驟中，像是在描述將大白菜分成四等分的時候，加入了不是用刀子切成四等分，而是在頭部切一小截後再撕成四等分，這也比較是韓國的作菜方式。另外還包含了像是以重物壓在大白菜上和適時的加上字，讓整體表達不會淪為生硬的作菜程序，可讀性可以更高。

Step 4　最後要提到的是句型變化，像這類的流程題目有很多，包含布或塑膠製成等，這類試題更難使用直條圖等的高階字彙去馬上描述出數值以獲取高分，加上不太好答，很可能看到題目就慌了。但是可以適時運用其他的句型而非簡單句型，讓作文更出色，例如可以使用動名詞當主詞的句型或是 To+ V..., S+V...等等的句型或是 before 或 after 的句型調整步驟順序，讓整體作文表達跟其他人不一樣，考生也可以自己試試看，組織出不一樣的範文。

經由先前的演練後，現在請看整篇範文並聆聽音檔

Given are diagrams about the procedures of making the simple Korean kimchi. Seven steps are included for making this prestigious dish. The first step involves evenly dividing the cabbage into quarters. It is advisable to cut the head for about an inch and split it into four parts by using hands, instead of using a knife. Salt is the key in the fermentation of the cabbage and sprinkle salt onto the cabbage leaves equally.

提供的圖表是關於製作簡易韓國泡菜的流程。製作這道享譽盛名的菜餚包含了七個步驟。第一個步驟是將大白菜均分成四等分。將大白菜頭切成約一寸並用手，而非使用刀子將其分成四份是更適當的方法。鹽是大白菜發酵的關鍵，並且將鹽均勻灑在白菜葉上。

The next step involves facilitation of the cabbage fermentation, so putting the heavy stuff onto the cabbage makes the fermentation rapider than letting it in a standstill. The fourth step is about removal of salt on these leaves and the cabbage can remain not salty and edible. To make it more palatable, ingredients are very important. These ingredients are made up of red pepper, an onion, garlic, and fish sauce. Using the blender to grind will make the paste smoother. Then comes the sixth step. Spreading the paste evenly onto the cabbage leaves until they are soaked with flavor. The final step will be putting the cabbage in the container in the refrigerator. After a week's magic fermentation, you will get the desired cabbage you want.

下一個步驟包含促成大白菜的發酵，所以要將重物壓在大白菜上，讓發酵更為快速，而非將其靜置。第四個步驟是移除這些葉子上的鹽份，使得大白菜能維持無鹽分且可供食用。為了讓其更為美味，原料也非常重要。這些成分是由紅辣椒、洋蔥、大蒜和魚露所組成的。使用攪拌機研磨會讓混合的糊更為順口。接著就是第六個步驟。將糊均勻分布在大白菜葉子上直到葉子都浸泡出風味。最後一個步驟是將大白菜放置在容器中並放入冰箱裡。在一個星期的魔力發酵後，你會得到你所想要的理想大白菜。

國家圖書館出版品預行編目(CIP)資料

雅思寫作聖經：小作文 / 韋爾著. -- 初版. --
新北市 : 倍斯特出版事業有限公司, 2022.
03　面；　公分. -- (考用英語系列 ; 037)
ISBN 978-626-95434-3-4(平裝)
1.CST: 國際英語語文測試系統 2.CST: 作文

805.189　　　　　　　　　111002369

考用英語系列　037

雅思寫作聖經-小作文（英式發音附QR Code音檔）

初　　版　　2022年3月
定　　價　　新台幣499元

作　　者　　韋爾
出　　版　　倍斯特出版事業有限公司
發 行 人　　周瑞德
電　　話　　886-2-8245-6905
傳　　真　　886-2-2245-6398
地　　址　　23558 新北市中和區立業路83巷7號4樓
E - m a i l　　best.books.service@gmail.com
官　　網　　www.bestbookstw.com
總 編 輯　　齊心瑀
特約編輯　　郭玥慧
封面構成　　高鍾琪
內頁構成　　菩薩蠻數位文化有限公司
印　　製　　大亞彩色印刷製版股份有限公司

港澳地區總經銷　　泛華發行代理有限公司
地　　址　　香港新界將軍澳工業邨駿昌街7號2樓
電　　話　　852-2798-2323
傳　　真　　852-3181-3973